Buck knew he shouldn't be thinking these thoughts about his brother's intended bride.

He shouldn't be noticing the light that shimmered in her hair. He shouldn't notice the gold flecks that danced in the uncommonly translucent hazel of her eyes, or the light sprinkle of freckles across the bridge of her button nose. He shouldn't notice those long coltish legs of hers or the shapely turn of her ankles. No, he shouldn't notice any of the things he'd spent the entire summer noticing about the completely captivating Holly Fergusson.

But he did. And he hated himself for it.

He had to get a hold of this fascination he had with his brother's fiancée before the guilt ate him alive.

He knew better than to want this woman the way he did.

But, he decided churlishly, it might be a hell of a lot easier to get her out of his mind if he knew his brother wanted her even half as much as he did.

Dear Reader,

The holiday season is a time for family, love...and miracles! We have all this—and more!—for you this month in Silhouette Romance. So in the gift-giving spirit, we offer *you* these wonderful books by some of the genre's finest:

A workaholic executive finds a baby in his in-box and enlists the help of the sexy single mom next door in this month's BUNDLES OF JOY, *The Baby Came C.O.D.*, by RITA Award-winner Marie Ferrarella. *Both* hero and heroine are twins, and Marie tells their identical siblings' stories in *Desperately Seeking Twin*, out this month in our Yours Truly line.

Favorite author Elizabeth August continues our MEN! promotion with *Paternal Instincts*. This latest installment in her SMYTHESHIRE, MASSACHUSETTS series features an irresistible lone wolf turned doting dad! As a special treat, Carolyn Zane's sizzling family drama, THE BRUBAKER BRIDES, continues with *His Brother's Intended Bride*—the title says it all!

Completing the month are *three* classic holiday romances. A world-weary hunk becomes *The Dad Who Saved Christmas* in this magical tale by Karen Rose Smith. Discover *The Drifter's Gift* in RITA Award-winning author Lauryn Chandler's emotional story. Finally, debut author Zena Valentine weaves a tale of transformation—and miracles—in *From Humbug to Holiday Bride*.

So treat yourself this month—and every month!—to Silhouette Romance!

Happy holidays,

Joan Marlow Golan
Senior Editor

Please address questions and book requests to:
Silhouette Reader Service
U.S.: 3010 Walden Ave., P.O. Box 1325, Buffalo, NY 14269
Canadian: P.O. Box 609, Fort Erie, Ont. L2A 5X3

HIS BROTHER'S INTENDED BRIDE

Carolyn Zane

Silhouette

R O M A N C E™

Published by Silhouette Books

America's Publisher of Contemporary Romance

For my darling mother- and father-in-law,
Gwen and John Pizzuti, who—thankfully—
in no way resemble George, Trudy, Miss Clarise
or Big Daddy!
THANK YOU
Judy, my sister and first-read editor;
this story was her brainchild.
And, as always, thank you to my sweet Lord.

 SILHOUETTE BOOKS

ISBN 0-373-19266-5

HIS BROTHER'S INTENDED BRIDE

This edition published by arrangement with Harlequin Books S.A.

® and TM are trademarks of Harlequin Books S.A., used under license.
Trademarks indicated with ® are registered in the United States Patent
and Trademark Office, the Canadian Trade Marks Office and in other
countries.

Printed in U.S.A.

CAROLYN ZANE

lives with her husband, Matt, and her toddler daughter, Madeline, in the scenic rolling countryside near Oregon's Willamette River. Like Chevy Chase's character in the movie *Funny Farm*, Carolyn finally decided to trade in a decade of city dwelling and producing local television commercials for the quaint country life of a novelist. And, even though they have bitten off decidedly more than they can chew in the remodeling of their hundred-plus-year-old farmhouse, life is somewhat saner for her than for poor Chevy. The neighbors are friendly, the mail carrier actually stops at the box, and the dog, Bob Barker, sticks close to home.

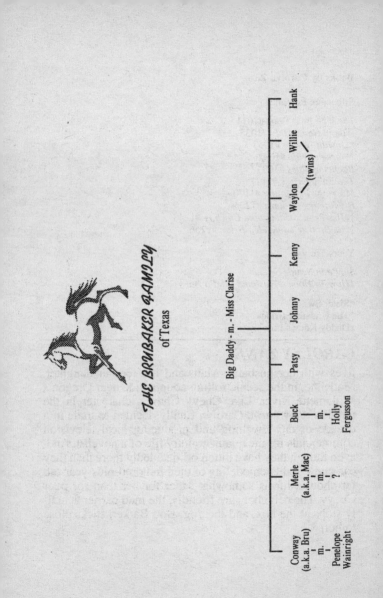

THE BRUBAKER FAMILY
of Texas

Big Daddy - m. - Miss Clarise

Conway (a.k.a. Bru) — m. — Penelope Wainright

Merle (a.k.a. Mac) — m. — ?

Buck — m. — Holly Fergusson

Patsy

Johnny

Kenny

Waylon — Willie (twins)

Hank

Prologue

"I think it's time we insisted that son of ours set a weddin' date, honey pie!" Big Daddy Brubaker stood on tiptoe and spread the library's window blinds with his stubby fingers. Pressing his nose into the opening he'd created, he peered outside and chortled with glee at the scene that met his eyes. "Just lookie there and see if you don't agree."

The diminutive patriarch of the large Brubaker clan was spying on Mac—no one called him by his given name of Merle—the second of his nine children. For, beyond the library window, on the sea of lawn that unfurled in front of the impressive Brubaker mansion, Mac and his lovely fiancée, Holly, were enjoying a game of croquet and—quite obviously—each other's company. Big Daddy reached behind his back, clasped the hand of his dubious wife and tugged her over to where he stood, fogging up the pane of glass.

"Yes, Big Daddy," Miss Clarise murmured. With a shake of her graying head, she watched her exuberant husband make a mishmash of the window blind as he attempted to reveal the loving display on the lawn for her inspection. "From all appearances, they do seem to be getting ready to set a date."

"Gettin' ready?" Tugging on the fringe of his leather jacket he struggled to extract it from the venetian blind's cords. "Why, just look at all that billin' and cooin' goin' on out there. I'd say our plan has worked perfectly."

"*Our* plan?" Miss Clarise frowned. She wanted no part of her husband's matchmaking schemes. Just because he'd been lucky with their oldest son, Bru, this past summer, was no reason to interfere in the rest of their children's lives.

"Well, of course," Big Daddy groused, flapping his fringe. "Our plan! The plan to marry off these kids of ours and get 'em out on their own. You saw how well it worked with Bru. Why, he and Penelope are happy as a couple of newly wedded clams! And now, a baby on the way!" he shouted, barely able to contain his zeal. "I can hardly wait! Soon I'll be bouncin' a little grandpuddin' on my knee!"

"Big Daddy," Miss Clarise cautioned, struggling to suppress the mirth that welled in her throat, "stop wiggling. You're going to pull the blind," she said and grimaced, "off the window..."

"No...I'm...not..." Big Daddy grunted and grappled with the elegant window treatment, only to become more hopelessly entangled. Lips pursed, he flailed until the brackets that held the window covering in place could no longer take the pressure and the blind—valance, brackets and all—came crashing down around his neck.

"Oops," he muttered. Looking sheepish, he glanced up at the couple on the lawn who now stood staring into the library window. With a lopsided smile, he poked his hand through the clattering panels and waved. Mac and Holly waved back, then embraced fondly before turning back to their game. "See?" His stage whisper filled the room. "Lookie, honey lips. Now *that's* what I call love."

Miss Clarise groaned and sagged against the heavy velvet draperies. Would Big Daddy never learn to stop meddling in his children's lives? She looked askance at her tiny husband of more than thirty years as he—his rubbery face wreathed in smiles—fondly watched his son play croquet with his fiancée.

To Big Daddy Brubaker, nothing was more sacred than family. It was very important to him that each of his offspring find the love and happiness that he'd found with Miss Clarise. They had nine children in all: Conway, who'd always answered to "Bru," Merle, whom everyone had dubbed "Mac," Buck, Patsy, Johnny, Kenny, the twins Waylon and Willie and last, but most certainly not least, young Hank. Much to their eternal chagrin, Big Daddy had insisted on naming all of his children after country music stars. For if there was one thing that Big Daddy enjoyed nearly as much as he enjoyed his family, it was country music.

However, country music aside, everything else in Big Daddy's life paled in comparison to the importance of his family, including his billion-dollar bank account, his rambling antebellum mansion known as the Circle B.O.—for Brubaker Oil—his thousands of acres of Texas ranch land, his half dozen vastly successful subsidiary companies or his many productive oil fields.

And now that Big Daddy's three oldest boys were all hitting their late twenties, he'd made it his primary goal in life to get his rowdy sons all polished up, hitched to nice girls and working on a passel of grandbabies for him to spoil. So far, Big Daddy had been lucky. Without even trying, he'd managed to get his oldest son, Bru, married off to Penelope Wainright, the plucky image consultant that he'd hired last summer to clean up his sons' images and get them ready for business and marriage. He hadn't expected to strike pay dirt quite so quickly, but no one could have been more pleased.

And now it looked as if Mac would soon be walking down the matrimonial trail after his brother, one short year later. Big Daddy hooked his thumbs on the clacking wooden panels that adorned his neck and sighed with happiness. It had been so easy! If he'd known how simple it was to have his renegade boys fall madly in love, he'd have started working on this little project ages ago.

This time all he'd done was put his head together with an old friend of the family, George Ferguson, and had him send his daughter, Holly, to spend the summer. Easy as pie. One minute, she and Mac were childhood playmates, and the next, they were quite obviously madly in love.

Nearly twenty years ago the Fergusons had been the Brubakers' closest neighbors and friends. Then George had struck oil on his Oklahoma spread, and moved his family north to tend his fields there. Over the years, the adults had vacationed together from time to time, but the kids hadn't seen one another since they were little tykes. After all these years Big Daddy knew he'd been taking a chance, inviting Holly to spend the summer. So much time had passed since she and Mac used to climb trees together as children. Why, he wasn't even sure they'd recognize each other, let alone begin to care so deeply.

But he'd been lucky in love once again, it seemed. The older man grew misty as a morning fog as he watched his strikingly handsome second son place a tender kiss on the lovely Holly Ferguson's cheek. Squeezing his raisinlike eyes tightly together, Big Daddy attempted to swallow past the poignant lump that filled his throat.

How wonderful. Soon, his family and the fine Ferguson family would be united in wedded bliss. In-laws. Mutual grandbabies. Oh, it was almost too good to be true. Sniffing, he blinked rapidly and struggled valiantly to pull himself together.

Making an unwieldy turn, Big Daddy snaked a finger through the blind he wore at his neck and pointed at the love of his life. "Sugar doll, let's call Mac in here and see if we can't get him to nail down a weddin' date. The sooner, the better, if we're gonna have another autumn weddin' extravaganza out in the gazebo. There are lists to make... Orders to place... People to notify..."

"Big Daddy, don't you think you're jumping the gun?"

Big Daddy shook his head, pooh-poohing his wife's concerns. "Not a chance, lamb doodle. Why, if you don't believe me, just look outside at those two lovebirds. Did you ever see such devotion?"

Slowly, Miss Clarise pulled back the heavy velvet drapes and peered uncertainly at her son. "They do seem quite...smitten."

Outside, Mac noticed his mother's gaze and lifted a hand in greeting.

"I told ya." Big Daddy chortled, and began to wrestle the blind from around his neck. "Where's my calendar, dumplin'? Let's go get Mac and we'll pick that date!"

Lifting her shoulders in resignation, Miss Clarise helped her husband free himself. "I don't know about this, Big Daddy."

"Oh, now, sugar. We don't want to stand in the way of true love, do we?"

"No," she murmured dubiously.

She didn't want to stand in the way of true love.

Chapter One

"Kiss me."

"Again?" Mac Brubaker exhaled noisily and, leaning forward, squinted at the wire wicket off in the distance.

Holly Ferguson pursed her lips at her fiancée's irritated tone. He needed to show a little more cooperation if they were going to make this work. "Yes, Mac darling," she instructed in a lackluster voice, "kiss me again."

"Just a sec," he promised, and waved a distracted hand behind his back at her, then aimed a stream of pithy expletives at yonder wicket.

Following his line of vision, Holly could see he had a lousy shot, but then the croquet mallet wasn't exactly his weapon of choice. Even so, he was playing as if the camera crew from the local sports station was hovering at his elbow. "I thought you said you hated croquet."

"I do."

"Well, your sudden fascination with the sport is interfering with our little...project."

"Okay, okay already."

"Hurry," she urged, darting a peek over her shoulder. "Just a quick one. On the cheek."

"Didn't we just do that?" Mac grumbled as he placed his hands on his thighs and pushed himself to a standing position.

"Yes, dear. And normally I wouldn't want to throw you off your game, but I think your folks are looking at us out the library window."

Mac straightened and tossed a covert glance toward the house. A groan resonated deep in his throat.

On tiptoe, Holly peeked over his shoulder and bit back a grin. Sure enough, Mac's father, who for some reason seemed hopelessly entangled in the window covering, was peering at them, waving and smiling broadly. Mac lifted a hand, returned the wave and, grabbing Holly's wrist, tugged her to his side.

"Oww, you big lummox," she complained testily, and offered him her cheek. "Easy on the arm. I only have two."

"Sorry," he murmured, managing to sound contrite. "I was just trying to look the part of the eager groom."

"Yeah, yeah, yeah." Clutching his arm for balance, she waited for him to kiss her.

Mac grinned and planted a noisy smack alongside her nose. "There," he said, releasing her arm and patting her lightly on the shoulder, "that oughta keep 'em happy."

"Yeech. Very funny." Wiping the damp spot on her nose with the back of her wrist, Holly tossed a bright smile over her shoulder toward Mac's curious father, then turned to follow Mac to the next wicket.

"I wonder how long we're going to have to keep this up." Mac sighed, his tone resigned, as they arrived at their shot.

Arching toward him, she gazed up into his face in a

practiced—if not totally adoring—fashion. "Until they give up and leave us alone."

Mac stoically returned her doe-eyed stare. "Fat chance."

Holly checked the library window once again from her peripheral vision. "Look alive. Your mother is watching." She exhaled wearily and waved.

"She is? Well, don't just stand there, hug me or something."

Complying in a halfhearted manner, Holly patted his back. "Okay. I think they saw that."

It was a beautiful day on a beautiful estate. The huge Brubaker antebellum mansion was breathtaking in both its style and enormity. Pillars, like sturdy sentinels, guarded the house proper, supporting what looked like acres of veranda on the first and second floors. The long driveway was lined with shade trees, and a half dozen other buildings dotted the surrounding area. From where she stood, Holly could clearly see the servants' quarters, a giant garage, the pool house, a gazebo, a greenhouse, the professionally manicured rose gardens and the stables. It was paradise. Perfect for romance. On any other day, with any other man, she might have been tempted to enjoy herself. But, alas, not today.

And most certainly not with this man who—at times like this—was far more infuriating than any older brother could be.

Mac straightened and gestured to the croquet mallet in her hands. "Your play, my little turtledove."

Ignoring his sarcasm, she leaned forward to line up her shot. As she did so, Mac flung a casual arm around her waist, then paused to give her derriere a few showy pats. Holly gasped and, with a wild swing, sent her ball rocketing across the driveway, down the gently sloping grassy knoll and toward the paddock, just outside the stable.

"For crying out loud, Mac," she muttered, sinking her elbow into his side. "That's not fair." She was growing weary of this game in more ways than one. It was a lucky thing they were such good pals or she would have been tempted to use her croquet mallet on his head.

Mac's grinning expression was irreverent. "Oh, yeah. Go on. Blame me for your lousy shot."

The bouncing ball seemed to sprout wings as it flew under the fence, across the muddy, manure-dotted horse paddock and into the stable.

"Oh, great. I guess I'm supposed to go get that." Holly's nose wrinkled in disdain as she glanced at her strappy sandals. "In these shoes."

An ear-to-ear grin—that made Holly want to slug him—split Mac's face as he gestured grandly toward the stable. "Be my guest."

With a snort of disgust, Holly shoved her mallet into his chest, gathered the gauzy skirt of her floral sundress and, whirling on her heel, set off to retrieve her ball. Trotting across the lawn, she skipped over the wide circular driveway and bounded down the grassy knoll to the split-rail fence. The gate, she discovered much to her chagrin, was about a mile away, on the opposite side of the paddock. As Holly stood studying her predicament, she decided it would be simpler and more efficient to simply climb over the stupid fence than to hike to the other side.

Irritated, she turned and stuck her tongue out at Mac as he lounged on the lawn, watching in lazy amusement. She wouldn't marry that grinning cretin even if their engagement were real, she thought churlishly as she bunched the skirt of her sundress into a wad and proceeded to climb—in a most undignified manner—over the filthy split rails.

Once she landed back on solid ground, Holly hippity-hopped between cow-pies, picking her way across the buzzing and odiferous arena until she finally made it to the stable's large double doors. Blinking rapidly in an effort to adjust to the sudden darkness, she thrust her hands in front of her and searched for her bearings. As she groped her way into the musty building, the smell of horse, hay and leather greeted her nose. Holly felt a broad smile bloom across her face as she peered into the gloaming. Nowhere did she revert to her childhood faster than in this horse barn. Dust floated slowly in the slanting rays of sunshine that filtered through the cracks in the barn's walls, illuminating the stalls and their curious occupants. Soft nickers and whinnies welcomed her, beckoning her to come rub a velvety nose.

An inch at a time, Holly worked her way down the barn's broad hallway until her hands came in contact with something warm and hard and...human? She jumped.

"Looking for something?" a low, masculine voice queried from the shadows at her side.

Spinning, Holly turned and squinted through the dim light into the face of Mac's younger brother, Buck.

"I—I, uh, yes," she stammered and, biting her lower lip, took a wobbly step back.

For the briefest of seconds their eyes locked, his dark, penetrating gaze looking into her soul, pricking her conscience. Nuts. Why did she have to run into him every time she turned around? Of all the people in the Brubaker family, Buck was the one who—even when they were children—she felt could see straight through her. Could read her mind.

The pensive expression on his face as he regarded her

now was so intense, it was almost as if he knew all about the whimsical little...pact she'd made with his older brother.

But that wasn't possible. Was it? Her heart fluttered in her chest and the blood flowed in a heated rush to her cheeks. Something about Buck and his deep, probing gaze made her feel transparent, and more than a little guilty.

Holly observed him through lowered lashes. She didn't remember feeling at all flustered around him when they used to play together as children in this barn. No, those had been carefree days, filled with laughter, friendship and the innocence of youth.

Unfortunately, Holly thought, waxing nostalgic as she noted the changes that had taken place in Buck, they were no longer children. The baby softness of his face had given way to the hard planes and lines of a masculine bone structure, and his smile, once so easy, was reserved now. But most unsettling of the changes in his appearance were his eyes.

All seeing. All knowing. Enigmatic.

A simple glance could have her quaking in her sandals and blithering like an idiot in mere seconds. It was maddening. Slowly he reached out and took her hand in his, and the warmth of his skin caused a flash of gooseflesh to snake up her arm. Dropping the croquet ball into her palm, he closed her fingers around the smooth surface and squeezed lightly.

"Here you go."

Her heart hammered. "I, uh, thank you," she mumbled, and gestured weakly toward the door. "I have to be getting back to, uh, you know, uh..." What was his name again?

Buck lazily lifted a brow as he studied her flushed cheeks.

"Mac," she croaked.

Rooted to the spot, she twisted the croquet ball nervously between her hands. As her eyes became used to the lack of light, Buck came into even sharper focus. It looked as if he'd just returned from riding the range, dressed as he was in faded blue jeans and a soft western shirt that did little to hide the power of his build.

"Your husband-to-be," he said, his tone lightly mocking.

"Uh, yes."

Still suffering the paralysis that came from standing beneath his gaze, she watched as he reached into his back pocket and fished out a well-worn pair of gloves. His motions were languid as he worked his fingers into the soft leather and flexed his hands to test the fit. Satisfied, he thumbed his Stetson farther back on his head, revealing the thick sandy hair that he shared with his two older brothers, then hooked his thumbs through his belt loops. Never once did he take his piercing stare from her face.

"Your—" his tone was irreverent "—intended. The love...of your life."

Slowly, ever so slowly, his upper lip curled, lifting the corners of his mouth, and Holly felt her temper flicker. Lips pursed in annoyance, her eyes dropped to his mouth. She couldn't tell in this light if he was grinning or smirking. This smug, aloof and slightly judgmental attitude of his was getting on her nerves.

Did he know or didn't he? This cat-and-mouse game was nerve-racking.

So far, Buck had been the hardest member of the family to become reacquainted with and, since her arrival here at the Circle B.O., he hadn't exactly been Mr. Warm and Welcoming. Not like the other Brubakers.

No one could say she hadn't tried with Buck. She had extended the hand of sisterly friendship. He had simply chosen to ignore it.

With an easy movement, he stretched and lightly scratched his broad chest. What was it about this grown-up version of her childhood pal, she wondered, watching as he settled against the wood slats that made up the stall at his back, that had her so ill at ease? As children, they'd been comfortable together. Hadn't they?

Yes. Of all the Brubaker offspring, Buck had changed the most. He was like a stranger now.

And surely, she thought with a clearing shake of her head, if she stood here and stared at him any longer, he would begin to think she was addle-brained. Reaching behind her, she groped for the wall and patted the boards in what she hoped was a breezy, carefree manner. She wasn't going to let him get her goat.

"Well," she chirped, walking backward into the sunshine to escape the building tension, "thanks again."

Buck simply cocked his head and shrugged.

"I have to get back to…you know…"

"Mac," he supplied, that infuriating, all-knowing look in his eyes.

"Yes. Mac," she whispered. Whirling on her heel, Holly flew outside.

Standing in the shadowed interior of the stable, Buck Brubaker watched as Holly hitched her skirt into a knot around her knees and began her thoroughly hypnotizing climb up the split-rail fence.

Have mercy, he thought on a heavy expulsion of breath. She sure had changed since they were little kids, chasing bullfrogs and fireflies together. Mac was a lucky son of a gun.

With a shake of his head, he tried to swallow past the sudden parched feeling in his mouth. Holly Ferguson had blossomed into an amazing woman. And such a pretty one, as well.

Honey brown in color, her silky straight hair framed her gamine face like a bouncy cloud, its length barely tickling her shoulders. As she reached the top rail, highlights shimmered in her thick, shiny mane as she tossed her head and paused for a moment in the bright summer sunshine to study the situation. It was clear she was trying to figure the best way to climb over the fence while doing the least amount of damage to the big flower-covered skirt of that filmy little outfit she wore.

Unable to help himself, Buck stood frozen to the spot and watched. What was it about his brother's fiancée that affected him this way? That had his blood rushing and his heart galloping. She wasn't really beautiful, not in the classical sense of the word, but there was a certain quality...a certain something that he found irresistible. She was adorable. Cute. Angelic in a perfectly devilish way. He found himself drawn to her zest for life, her dry, witty sense of humor and her adventuresome spirit, like no other woman before. It had been a constant battle, staying away from her this summer. Something about Holly clicked deep in his soul. Like the missing piece to a puzzle, when he was in her presence, he felt complete. Happy. Excited.

Miserable.

Pushing himself away from the stall wall, he flexed his hands within his gloves and felt a sense of shame fill his belly. He shouldn't be thinking these thoughts about his brother's woman.

It wasn't right.

He shouldn't be noticing the light that shimmered in her hair. He shouldn't notice the way she worried her full lower lip with the tip of her tongue. He shouldn't notice the gold flecks that danced in the uncommonly translucent hazel of her eyes, or the light sprinkle of freckles across the bridge of her button nose. He shouldn't notice the long coltish length of her legs or the shapely turn of her ankles. No, he shouldn't notice any of the things he'd spent the entire summer noticing about the completely captivating Holly Ferguson.

But he did.

And he hated himself for it.

With a disgusted snort, he raked a gloved hand across his face and shook his head. He had to get ahold of this little fascination he had with his brother's fiancée before the guilt ate him alive.

He needed to get a life. To start seriously dating somebody else. Anybody else. Lifting his eyes, he allowed his gaze to follow Holly's progress as she approached his brother.

He knew better than to want this woman the way he did.

But, he decided churlishly, it might be a hell of a lot easier to get her out of his mind if he knew Mac wanted her even half as much as he did.

"What took you so long?" Mac grumbled, gesturing toward the house. "Big Daddy nearly gave himself a concussion on the library window, trying to see where you'd run off to."

Handing Holly her croquet mallet, Mac dramatically draped a possessive arm around her waist and slyly checked the library window.

"I can't play if you're going to hold me so tight," she groused, and, glancing toward the stable, felt suddenly uncomfortable with Mac's flamboyant embrace. Buck was nowhere in sight, but still, for reasons she couldn't begin to describe, Holly didn't like the idea that he might be watching. Shaking loose from Mac's grip, she moved away and took a deep breath. "No wonder I'm losing."

Noting her agitation, he guffawed. "Sorry. I must have been getting carried away with my role. You have to admit, though, since we've been going along with this whole engagement thing, our parents have stopped nagging us about settling down and getting married, and have blessedly stopped digging up people for us to date."

"True." Holly dropped the croquet ball on the lawn and sighed. "That is amazing, considering my folks are every bit as bad as yours when it comes to meddling." She glanced back at the stable. No one was in sight and she began to relax again.

Mac's snort was incredulous. "I find that hard to believe."

"Trust me, they are. You'll see when they come to visit in a few weeks to get reacquainted with their future son-in-law." She pursed her lips to stem a tide of laughter at his pained expression.

Mac groaned.

"You don't remember the real George and Trudy Ferguson. You were just a little kid, last time you saw them. You don't remember how determined they can be when they set their minds to something," she gloomily prophesied. "Especially when it comes to getting their only child married off to the right man from the right family."

Nervously, she worked her diamond engagement ring around in circles on her slender finger. Trust her folks to come swooping down from Oklahoma for a celebratory visit. Once again, she wondered about the sanity of this little plan.

Settling the croquet mallet across the nape of his neck, Mac looped his wrists over the wooden handle and pulled a thoughtful face. "You know, that's something we didn't exactly think all the way through when we got engaged at the beginning of the summer. I mean, how," he wondered aloud, arching a curious brow in Holly's direction, "and when, exactly, are we going to break it to them that we're not in love?"

Holly rubbed her suddenly throbbing temples. Thoughts of her meddling parents routinely gave her a tension headache. "Good question. I still haven't figured that part out yet. It seemed like such a good idea when we decided to turn the tables on them and shock their shoes off by getting engaged."

The idea had been to teach the well-intentioned foursome a lesson. When Holly had arrived at the ranch in early June, she'd been relieved to discover that Mac was just as disgusted as she was with being a pawn in an arranged marriage. Jokingly, she'd suggested they go along with their parents wishes on the surface, and simply enjoy the summer doing as they pleased. Together, Holly had reasoned, she and Mac would be able to find relief from the endless nagging of four loving—albeit over-zealous—parents.

Amazingly enough, Mac had jumped at the idea and, for reasons she hadn't yet puzzled out, seemed eager for the refuge this loveless partnership would provide.

Unfortunately, neither had figured on the subtle pressure to set a wedding date and begin making the million and one wedding plans their somewhat less than serious engagement would bring. Nor had they counted on the idea that, to their parents anyway, engagement would mean marriage. And sooner, it seemed, rather than later. Holly sighed heavily.

If there was one thing she did not want at this juncture of her life, it was marriage. Contrary to her parents' gloomy opinion, at twenty-seven years old she still considered herself to be young. Holly had always had a long list of very important accomplishments she hoped to achieve in her life, before she settled into the role of wife and mother. She wanted to make a contribution to society that had nothing to do with her father or his money. Accomplishments that her oil tycoon father just couldn't seem to understand.

Besides, if and when she truly became engaged to be married, it would be to a man of her own choosing. A man she fell madly in love with. A man who shared her dreams and interests. Not someone her father insisted upon. Not someone handpicked because of his pedigree. Most certainly not Mac Brubaker. And, luckily, Mac seemed to feel the same way about her.

At the time, getting engaged had seemed like the perfect solution. For everyone. Unfortunately, the complications were beginning to multiply. How would their little ruse hold up under George and Trudy Ferguson's scrutiny?

Holly lifted her eyes to Mac's and sighed. "I thought getting engaged would simplify our lives."

A muscle jumped in Mac's jaw. "Yeah, well, it's anything but simple. For either of us."

She studied his haunted expression, wishing for the millionth time that he would share whatever was bothering him. But they didn't have that kind of relationship.

And like it or not, that's the way it was. Try as she might to fulfill her parents' wishes and fall in love with the second Brubaker son, it simply wasn't meant to be.

There was no spark. No thrill. No...attraction. Not that she didn't find Mac attractive. He was perfectly handsome and—when he wanted to be—charming. That wasn't the problem. They simply weren't suited.

Unfortunately, like her parents before her, Holly was beginning to wonder, as she and Mac strolled across the rolling lawn toward their next shot, if she would ever find the man that could make her heart pound. Her blood roar. Her pulse sing. Her...toes...curl...

Holly's feet slowed as she suddenly felt the little hairs at the back of her neck begin to tingle. *Buck.* She was developing a sixth sense where he was concerned. Without looking toward the barn, she could feel his eyes upon her once again. Why was he always there, hawking her every move? she wondered anxiously. His probing gaze made her positively antsy.

"What's wrong?" Pausing, Mac turned and waited for her to catch up.

"Nothing. It's just that I think...someone's—" she paused and drew her lower lip into her mouth "—watching us."

"Aww, man. Again?" Mac sighed, stopping in his tracks and planting his hands at his hips. "What should we do this time? Do you have any ideas? We should probably keep it creative to be convincing, don't you think?"

"No. That's not necessary. We don't need to do anything like that, really, it's just that I—"

"Yeah, you're right." Moving back toward her, he took her hand and pulled her next to him. "Let's just get it over with."

While Mac planted yet another platonic kiss in the vicinity of her cheek, the squirming Holly caught a movement near the barn. Her heart stood still as her gaze collided with Buck's. Lingering for a moment in the shadows just inside the main horse barn's broad double doors, he watched her, an unfathomable look on his ruggedly handsome face.

Holly tried unsuccessfully to swallow.

After skipping several successive beats, her heart began to race, forcing the blood to roar in her ears. He knew. She could just tell by the way he was looking at her...he knew. She blinked and clutched at Mac's shirt as her knees went suddenly weak.

"Hey," Mac said with an easy grin. "You're getting kind of convincing at this little game of ours. But take it easy on the buttons, will you?"

"Sorry." Holly shook her head to clear it. "I guess I'm getting tired, or something," she said by way of explanation.

"We could quit, if you want," Mac offered, supporting her arms with his hands. "I understand. You have taken quite a beating..." he goaded her good-naturedly.

"No, that's okay. Let's finish the game. For appearances." Unable to control the direction of her gaze, Holly's eyes strayed of their own volition toward the shadowed entrance to the barn.

Buck was gone.

Well...good.

What did she care if Buck wanted to shake her confidence? She would simply ignore him and his smug little attitude. She didn't have to worry about him. She was engaged to his older brother, for heaven's sake. Well, okay, technically not, but no one knew that but her and Mac. She hoped. At any rate, no matter how bogus her relationship with Mac may be, falling to a pile of twittery pieces every time Buck glanced her way would never do.

She had to get a grip. Maybe tonight, after dinner, she

and Mac could figure out what they were going to do with the rest of their lives and then plan their devastating breakup. That ought to buy them both some more time to pursue their individual dreams. This way, she could make good her escape in the near future, to ostensibly nurse her bruised and broken heart for several years. In theory, the plan was sound.

But for now anyway, she simply wasn't up for such a mind-bending discussion.

Grinning at Mac, Holly playfully brandished her croquet mallet and attempted to throw off her mild funk. Ever fun loving, she was not one to sit around and stew about circumstances. Life was meant to be enjoyed, no matter how wearisome the situation.

"Race you to the next wicket," she drawled, and proceeded to stroll lazily past Mac.

"You're on." Mac's voice was loaded with good-natured sarcasm as he shouldered his mallet and sauntered after her.

"Mac, darlin'," Miss Clarise's soft Southern drawl reached them from the front steps of the veranda.

Mac paused. "Yes, ma'am?"

"Big Daddy was wondering if you could join him in the library for a moment to consult with his calendar?"

"Yes, ma'am." Mac sighed. Turning to face Holly he muttered, "Consult with his calendar? Uh-oh. Sounds like they want us to set a wedding date."

"Think so?" Her brow creased with concern. "What are you going to do?"

"Don't worry," he assured her. "I'll think of something."

"I hope so." Holly sighed as she watched her intended trot across the lawn toward the house. "I sure hope so."

* * *

She was alone.

Again.

For a couple who claimed to be in love, they sure didn't spend much time together. This farcical croquet game was the first time they'd spent more than a moment or two together for over a week.

Buck's hands slowed as he coiled a length of rope around his arm. He could see Holly, standing on the lawn, silhouetted against the soft afternoon light that filtered through the shade trees. The flowery skirt she wore had become translucent in this light, revealing the shapely curve of her lithe figure. She seemed deep in thought as she strolled over to an iron bench that sat nestled against a long row of English box hedge. Slowly she lowered herself into the seat, crossed her legs and leaned back to absorb a little summer sun.

Buck grinned in spite of the four-alarm fire that was consuming his gut. So that's where those little freckles that danced across her cheeks and nose had come from.

Shouldering one coil of rope, he glanced around for his brother. Nowhere in sight, as usual. With a shake of his head, Buck snorted and tossed another rope over a peg on the wall. Why wasn't Mac dying to spend every waking moment with her? he wondered. He sure as heck was, and she wasn't even his bride-to-be. Turning, he moved to the double doors, stared out into the sunshine and debated. Nah. This was stupid. Who cared if she was being neglected by his thoughtless brother?

Leave her alone, boy, the rational side of his mind commanded.

Go talk to her, the foolhardy side of his mind urged.

Buck flexed his hands at his sides as he allowed his conscience to do battle with his heart.

Since the day she'd arrived, he'd been pretty good

about steering clear of her, except for the multitude of times when they'd accidentally bumped into each other in passing. Surely it wouldn't hurt to run over and make a friendly comment or two about the weather. Being that his brother had obviously left her to her own devises.

Maybe, he thought as his feet began to carry him across the paddock to the fence, maybe if he talked to her for a moment, he could get on with his day and stop thinking about her. That made sense, he thought as he scaled the fence and leapt to the other side. Straightening his legs, he stamped his feet on the ground and pushed his jeans back down his lanky legs and over his boots where they belonged. Then he dusted off his shirt and ran a hand through his hair.

Don't play with fire, boy, the rational side of his mind commanded.

Just talk to her, the foolhardy side of his mind urged.

Criminy. Why was he being such an idiot? Holly was no mystery woman. She was the same girl who used to eat mud pies with him and his sister when they were little. She just didn't look the same, that's all. Time to debunk the mystery, he thought, and strode with determination across the lawn to where she sat on the wrought-iron bench. Yeah, she was just another dirt-and-bug-eating kid from his childhood. Not the goddess he'd built her up in his mind to be.

At his approach, Holly opened her eyes and tilted her head toward him, and Buck felt the color drain from his face. Oh, great balls of fire. She was the goddess he'd built her up in his mind to be.

A slow smile tipped her full lips as she looked up at him curiously. Her lashes created long shadows across her cheeks, and her hair—oh, that wonderful hair that he longed to fill his hands with—was spun gold in this light.

Get the hell outta here, boy, his rational mind cautioned.

Get the hell outta here, boy, his foolhardy mind screamed.

Holly leveraged herself upright on the seat and gazed up at him, a quizzical look on her heart-shaped face.

"Hi," she said in that soft, velvety alto voice that drove him wild.

"You seen a weather report?" he barked rudely.

"Uh…" she stammered, taken back by his gruff manner. "I think it's supposed to be sunny till the end of the week."

Without even acknowledging her gracious assistance, Buck grunted, spun on his heel and stormed back to the relative safety of the barn.

"You're here! Hot diggity," Big Daddy exclaimed, and, finally free of his venetian neck ornament, rushed across the library to greet his second son. "Noticed ya out there, having a little game of croquet with your intended," he thundered happily. Gesturing to a wine-colored wingback chair, he motioned for Mac to take a seat. "Sit, sit, sit," ordered the diminutive man.

"You noticed that, did you?" Mac asked dryly. Stepping over the mangled wooden venetian blind on his way to the chair, he settled into his seat and regarded his father's glowing face.

"And how. You and Miss Holly there seem thicker than a molasses milkshake."

"Mmm" was Mac's noncommittal response.

Big Daddy gleefully slapped his thigh and crowed with jubilation. "Well, that's just fine. We're happy for ya, son." His face was wreathed in wrinkles of joy. "Anywho, your mother and I have been thinkin'." The older man lifted his leather-bound business calendar off his desk and, tucking it under his arm, moved toward the wingback chairs near the fireplace, where his son was already seated.

"You have?" Mac glanced around the elegantly appointed library for Miss Clarise, but she had disappeared, as she was wont to do whenever her husband began to stick his nose where it didn't belong.

"Yep," Big Daddy crowed and, giving himself a little running start, hop, skipped and jumped into the wingback chair across from Mac. Snatching a cigar out of a box on the coffee table, the tiny man leaned back, stuffed the expensive Cuban stogie into the corner of his mouth and trained his hawkish gaze on his son. "We've been thinkin' that you two little lovebirds should pick out a wedding date."

"You…have."

"Yep." The older man pulled his calendar from under his arm and flipped it open to the months at the end of that summer. "We've been thinkin' that September might be nice. That's only a month or so away. Plenty of time to plan big doin's, like we did for Bru and Penelope. We've been thinkin' that the sooner you two get this date thing settled, the smoother everything will go." Withdrawing a pen from his breast pocket, Big Daddy's expression was expectant as he stared at his second son.

Mac sighed in exasperation. "And what about what we think?" he burst out. "Big Daddy, did you ever stop to consider that?"

Yanking his cigar from the corner of his mouth, Big Daddy brandished it in energetic circles as he squinted at Mac. "Well, now. What's the holdup?" he countered. "You're in love. You're engaged." He thrust his calendar out in front of him. "Pick a date."

"Auggh," Mac groaned. Leaping to his feet, he planted his hands on his hips and towered over his father.

Fortunately, before he could unleash the years of frustration that crowded into his throat, Miss Clarise interrupted. "Mac, darlin', this telegram just came for you." Gracefully crossing the highly polished hardwood of the library floor, she extended the yellow missive toward her son. "Here you go, sweetheart."

"*Telegram?*" Big Daddy thundered. "Who would send a telegram in this day and age of computers and fax machines?"

Rolling his eyes, Mac shook his head. Grateful for the reprieve, he ripped open the telegram and read it. As his eyes moved over the words, his demeanor changed in a way that was nearly palpable in its electricity. His mouth dropped and his eyes glazed over. Then his jaw hardened and his eyes became steely.

"Well," Big Daddy demanded, "who's it from?"

Crumpling the telegram, Mac stuffed it into his pocket and, without a backward glance, strode rapidly across the room to the door.

His brow knitted into a quizzical caterpillar, Big Daddy stared after his son's rapidly retreating form. "Mac!" he hollered at the top of his lungs. "Mac! Where you goin'?"

Barley pausing, Mac called over his shoulder in a grim voice. "I have to go."

"Where?"

"On a little trip." Yanking open the closet door, he retrieved a bag that he'd packed for just such an occasion.

"But when will you be back?"

"I'll let you know when I find out." Mac's voice grew dim as he reached the front door. "Expect me when you see me."

"But...but... Now listen here..." Big Daddy sputtered, his jaw slack, his furry brows now sky-high.

The door slammed with a resounding crash of finality, and from his vantage point at the library window, Big Daddy could see his son striding across the lawn toward his waiting fiancée.

"What in tarnation is goin' on around here?" the older man demanded, pressing his nose to the glass pane and taking in the look of surprise that crossed Holly's face as Mac spoke rapidly to her.

"I don't know, Big Daddy," Miss Clarise murmured, and, pulling the silk tasseled cord, began to draw the heavy velvet draperies. "But for once, may I suggest that you keep your nose out of it."

Chapter Two

"*Married?*"

Had she heard correctly? Jaw hanging slack, Holly watched in amazement as Mac bounded across the lawn and—not bothering to open the door—grabbed the roll bars and swung himself into his convertible Jeep. Then, throwing it into reverse, he spun in a dangerous circle, impatiently ground the gears and proceeded to tear down the driveway with nary a backward glance.

He was already married?

Feeling as if she'd just been sucker punched by a torpedo, all Holly could do was stare after his dusty wake and gasp for oxygen. What the heck was she supposed to do now? she wondered dumbly as her entire reason for being at the Circle B.O. and his shiny black Jeep zoomed down the driveway and out of the picture.

Mac was married. Married. Married.

The words reverberated in her head, and she listened to them echo, trying to digest their meaning. Good heavens! Her fiancé was married to another woman, and he expected her to not only keep this fact a secret, but to carry on with the charade. She bit back the hysterical urge to laugh. This ridiculous hole just got deeper all the time.

"Whatever you do," Mac had instructed, his voice grim with warning, "don't say *anything* to *anybody* about this till I get back." Reaching out, he'd tipped her chin and looked into her face. "Promise me."

Brow wrinkled incredulously, Holly had looked at him as if he'd lost his faculties. "How can I say anything, when I don't have any idea what you're talking about?" she'd accused, poking him in the chest with her fingertips.

"Listen," Mac had ground out, plunging his hands through his hair. "I don't have time to tell you the whole story right now, but I swear I'll tell you everything just as soon as I get back. Promise me, Holly. Promise me you won't tell anyone about this. This is critical to my future. I don't want my family jumping in to save the day, and possibly ruining everything."

"What everything? What are you talking about? When did you get married? Who did you get married to? Where has she been all summer? Why—"

Mac had held up a palm to deflect her rapid-fire questions. "Look, Holly, I gotta go. It's an…emergency. Just promise you won't say anything. Promise."

His tone had been urgent, the look in his eye desperate. Obviously, whatever was going on in his life was extremely important to him. How could she refuse him, when he'd spent the entire summer going along with her little…practical joke? Like it or not, she owed him. Mac Brubaker had been a good friend to her this summer. As much as she hated the idea of continuing this downward spiral of lies, she couldn't—at this particular mind-blowing juncture, anyway—think of another plan. She deserved every bit of what she was getting. And, unfortunately, it wasn't over yet.

Far too late in the game she was realizing what the truth could do to the people she'd come to care a great deal for. Visions of Big Daddy's cheerful face flashed in her mind. Maybe she wasn't going to marry Mac, but strangely enough, she felt like a part of his giant, loving family.

"Okay. Okay." She'd groaned and tried to ignore the sudden stabbing pain in her temples. "I promise. Just don't leave me twisting in the wind forever, okay?"

Relief had flooded his face. He'd grasped her hands in a parting squeeze. "I'll try not to."

"When will you get back?"

"I don't know." Shaking his head, Mac had dropped her hands and started walking backward, then running, toward his Jeep. "Several weeks at least," he'd called. "Maybe more. There are some unexpected...complications. Thanks, Holly. Being engaged to you was fun. But more importantly, it may have saved my marriage."

"Glad I could help," she'd drawled as he'd driven off.

Complications. Ha. That was an understatement. And now, thanks to the soft spot in her head, she was left holding the bag. But, she thought as she massaged her throbbing temples, he'd looked so shell-shocked, standing there with his heart on his sleeve, she couldn't have refused him if she'd wanted. Closing her eyes, a moan generated in the pit of her stomach and escaped on a sigh past her lips. Well, she thought resignedly, she would simply have to deal with the complications on this end. Because there would be complications aplenty.

Holly's forlorn gaze traveled unseeing across the lawn.

What in heaven's name was she supposed to do for the next several weeks? she wondered anxiously. How was she supposed to keep this wacky engagement of theirs up all by herself? And what on earth was she supposed to tell her mother and father when they arrived to welcome their future son-in-law into the bosom of their family? Oh, good heavens. Panic began to swirl in her stomach and claw its way into her throat. And...and...and what if they arrived before Mac did? This was simply terrible.

Another disturbing thought flitted through Holly's befuddled mind as she stood there, trying to organize her jumbled thoughts.

"Buck." As she whispered his name, a current of fear shimmied up her spine. He would know the game she was playing for sure now. He would certainly be able to see right through her, especially now that Mac wasn't there to shield her from Buck's dark, all-seeing eyes.

Taking a deep breath, Holly tried to control the fit of hyperventilation she felt coming on. She would have to avoid Buck. Yes. That would be simple enough, wouldn't it?

Oh, who was she trying to kid? Good grief. She was living under the same roof with the man. She couldn't avoid him forever. Especially since every time she turned around, she seemed to bump into him.

Holly covered her face with her free hand and felt a bubble of hysterical laughter begin to build in her belly. This was insane. Her life was such a pathetic shambles. When had she allowed herself to sink so incredibly low? Two months ago this whole crazy idea had seemed so wonderful. A lark. A little prank, simply meant to put four interfering people in their place. A practical joke.

And now? The joke was on her. Now she was stuck in a phony engagement for the rest of the summer to plan a wedding that wouldn't happen, with a fiancé who was missing in action, not to mention married to another woman.

"Ohh," she giggled, her shoulders bobbing with the ridiculousness of it all. Tears of mirth gathered in her eyes and she swiped at them with the back of her hand as they began to flow down her cheeks. Clutching her sides, she allowed the laughter to flow, knowing if she didn't, she would start to cry.

Was she crying?

It was none of his business.

Trying to look busy, Buck needlessly inspected several more coils of new rope he'd purchased only the day before, and covertly studied Holly. As he leaned against the old parade wagon that sat in the paddock, he angled his head such that he could see her from beneath the brim of his Stetson without being detected. Lifting his gaze from the forlorn figure who cut such a heart-wrenching figure on the lawn, he scowled down the driveway, and tried to stifle the urge to run to her aid.

Where was Mac? Why had he driven off like a bat out of hell that way? Did they have a fight? And, most importantly, *was* she crying? Something sharp twisted in his gut.

It wasn't any of his business, he sternly reminded himself again.

Even so, he'd have to be blind not to notice the way she was clutching her little croquet mallet, her head bowed, her shoulders shaking with emotion. The muscles in Buck's jaw jumped as a surge of protectiveness seared his brain. His idiot brother didn't know what a good thing he had. That much was obvious by the way he'd been treating Holly. From his limited observations, it was clear from the get-go that Mac's feelings for Holly weren't what they should be. Why, if she were his, Buck thought fiercely as he bent to retrieve another coil of rope from the ground, he'd treat her like a queen. But she wasn't his. Never would be.

Shouldering the rope, Buck ripped his eyes away from Holly and strode back into the stable's shadowed interior. If Mac didn't watch his p's and q's, he just might lose her. And that would be a terrible loss. Buck loved his brother like...well, like a brother. But that was no excuse for his apathetic behavior all summer. When that sorry excuse for a fiancé came home, Buck was going to have a word or two with him about the proper care and maintenance of a woman like Holly.

"There ya are," Big Daddy's voice boomed down the stable's broad corridor, drawing Buck from his ruminations and back to the present.

"You looking for me?" Buck's tone was a little edgier than he meant for it to be. Turning, he watched his father stride across the hay-covered slats that made up the floor.

"Yeah." As he reached his son, Big Daddy planted his hands on his hips and squinted up.

Buck sighed. He'd seen that look on his father's face before. "What's going on?"

"I don't rightly know. Thought maybe you could help. Any idea what's wrong with that dunderheaded Mac? He say anything to you about a mid-life crisis?"

"What do you mean?" A scowl marred his brow. His brother wasn't even thirty yet. How could it be a mid-life crisis? It was true, however, that Mac had been acting strange for the better part of a year now. Lapsing into stony silences, a hair-trigger temper and becoming suddenly engaged to Holly, a woman he didn't seem to be passionately in love with, among myriad other things that weren't his usual happy-go-lucky self. Something was different all right, but nothing that his brother couldn't work out on his own.

"Well, I was talking to Mac back at the house a few minutes ago about settin' a weddin' date for him and Holly."

Buck folded his arms across his chest, in an attempt to contain his inner turmoil. "So?"

Agitated, Big Daddy began to pace. "So a telegram arrived for him, and then, without so much as a by-your-leave, he up and left. Holly told me just now that he'll be gone for several weeks at least. Several weeks," Big Daddy shouted. "What in blue blazes is that all about?"

Buck's head snapped up. "Did Holly give a reason?"

"Look at her, boy!" Big Daddy pointed at the pathetic figure on the lawn. "She was so overcome by emotion, I could barely understand her. Crying her sweet little head off, the tears were simply pourin' down her cheeks."

Opening and closing his fists, Buck forced himself to stay put. This is none of your business, the words echoed like a mantra in his mind.

"Anywho, from what I could gather from her, Mac said something about needin' some time away to adjust to married life. Have you ever heard of such a thing?" the old man roared. "Sounds like a plain old case of lily-livered cold feet to me."

Buck frowned. "Time...away?"

"Tell me about it," Big Daddy ranted. "Your poor mama is scandalized! This no way for a Brubaker to behave! That's why I need your help."

"My help?"

"Yep. I need you to entertain Miss Holly until that cowardly coyote of a brother of yours gets back."

"Me?" Buck felt the blood drain from his face. "Oh, now wait just a minute…"

"Yes, you! You're the only choice. Bru and Penelope don't have time, with the baby comin', and your sister won't be back from Europe for a while yet. The other boys are too young to understand the sensitive nature of this predicament, you follow? We can't let her get away just because that snake-bellied son of mine is goin' through some kind of prenuptial jitters! We have to make her feel welcomed into the bosom of our family. That's your job, boy."

"Oh, no, you don't." Buck's voice was grim as he held up a hand to silence his sputtering father. "Now hold on just a damn minute. I don't see how this is my problem. This is between Ho—"

"Of course this is your problem! This is about family!" Spinning on his heel, Big Daddy yanked off his hat and pointed it at his son. "Talk to her, boy! Get to know her! Take her to a party or a dance. Introduce her to some of the young people in the area. After all, in a month or two, you'll be sister and brother. It's time you two got reacquainted after all these years. She's not the little kid you used to skinny-dip with out there in the cattle tanks."

I'll say, Buck thought grimly, darting a glance through the double doors to where Holly was still standing on the lawn, obviously in agony. And that was precisely the point. They weren't little kids anymore. The muscle in his jaw twitched as he tore his eyes from Holly and rested them on his father.

"No. Forget it, Big Daddy. I don't think I should be spending that much time with Mac's fiancée."

"Horsefeathers! You have to admit, you haven't made much effort to socialize with her. Not like the rest of the family. She's gonna think you don't like her."

Buck groaned.

It was true. He had been avoiding her, but for reasons he could never admit to his father. If Big Daddy thought he was scandalized now, he'd probably go to his heavenly reward over the feelings his third son had for the woman on the lawn. "I have work to do, Big Daddy! I can't just drop everything and go—"

"Fiddlesticks. This place can run itself for a few weeks and you know it. That's what we have all these hired hands for. Run and get cleaned up and then go talk to that poor girl. Give her a shoulder to cry on. I think she's too proud to spill her guts to me or your mama. You go try and figure out what's wrong."

"I'm telling you, I don't think this is such a good idea."

"It's our only idea. Go on, boy, and that's an order." Eyes narrowing, Big Daddy pulled his trump card. "Buck, you know you owe Mac for that time he dragged you outta the cow tank where you were foolin' around and almost drowned yourself as a kid. He saved your sorry hide, boy! The least you can do is entertain his little missus for a few measly weeks till he gets his head screwed on straight." Arching a rubbery brow, Big Daddy narrowed keen eyes on his son and roared. "Don't give me any grief, Buck. Just do it!"

Buck could only stare at his father as the older man ranted. Big Daddy had him over a barrel, and he knew it. How could he refuse? He wouldn't even be standing here if it wasn't for his brother. Dammit, anyway. For the first time in his life, he wished Mac had left him breathing sludge at the bottom of the cow tank all those years ago.

His stomach churning, his gaze slowly wandered over to Holly once again. She'd sunk to the ground and was using the hem of her gauzy skirt to dab her tears. Squeezing his eyes tightly shut, Buck groaned. Aw, man. He was in trouble. Big trouble.

"We're all countin' on ya here. Specially that little gal out there, cryin' her heart out." Big Daddy jabbed a hand into his graying hair and, tugging in frustration, spun around and proceeded to march out of the barn, muttering all the while. "I'm tellin' ya." The old man's diatribe continued, wafting back and growing dim as he disappeared. "You boys are gonna be the death of me for sure, one of these days..."

Buck lifted his head to the sky and he implored the heavens for help. To Buck's way of thinking, it was the other way around.

For surely Big Daddy would be the death of him.

"Here you go."

Prying her fingers away from her eyes, Holly looked up to find a glass of iced tea cradled in a masculine hand, hovering just in front of her nose. *Buck.* She hadn't sensed his presence this time. But then her radar was probably a little off, being that she'd just spent the past hour walking aimlessly around the yard, alternately laughing hysterically and cursing Mac's name.

"Thank you," she murmured, taking the cool, sweating glass in her hands and pressing it to the cheeks she knew were red and blotchy from her outburst of hilarity. Thankfully she was back in control of her senses. She peeked up at him and her mouth went dry. Okay, maybe not all of her senses, but most of them.

"Mind if I join you?" Buck asked, his low voice carrying a sympathetic note.

Not waiting for her reply, he grasped the ornate hand railing and took the last step up into the old Victorian gazebo. She finally settled here after her walk, choosing to sit and contemplate her situation on one of the two porch swings.

Yes, she minded. She was skittish enough without adding Buck's probing gaze to her anxiety level. However, short of walking away, what choice did she have?

"Sure," she heard herself say in spite of her better judgment. Gathering her skirt, she pushed it aside and made room for him on the swing. Maybe she could exchange a few pleasantries, then make an excuse to get away from him. She could feel his eyes roving curiously over her, leaving a tingling path in their wake.

She was dead meat.

Already the jig was up, and Mac hadn't been gone an hour yet. Locking her gaze on the crisscrossing straps of her sandals, Holly avoided looking into his eyes. Now, more than ever, she felt transparent and vulnerable to Mac's astute younger brother.

"You okay?" he asked softly.

Shifting her gaze, she eyed the crisp creases in his gabardine slacks. He'd changed his clothes. Absently, she wondered why.

"Sure," she said with a shrug that she hoped conveyed a spirit of carefree abandon. "Why do you ask?" She flashed a bright smile in the direction of his solid chest. The shirt he wore fit like a favorite pair of soft gloves, contouring snugly to the hills and valleys of his rangy, athletic build.

"No particular reason." His ice cubes tinkled in his glass as he took a sip of his tea. "It's just that Big Daddy mentioned Mac had to leave for a few days—"

"Weeks," she interrupted. Might as well set him straight on that from the get-go. She was in enough hot water without everyone constantly asking her when Mac was going to reappear.

"Weeks..." he repeated. The curiosity in his voice was hard to mistake.

"Uh, yes."

Holly touched her tongue to her lower lip. As they rocked to and fro, his body rested lightly against hers at the thigh and bicep. She could feel the energy crackling between the two of them, and attributed it to the fact that Buck had some kind of X-ray vision where she was concerned. Blinking rapidly, she leaned away. She had to fight this power he seemed to have over her.

"Yes." Stalling, she groped her mind for a plausible explanation that wouldn't betray Mac. "Uh-huh." She nodded. "Weeks. More than one. W-week, that is," she stammered.

"Where did he go?" Casually, Buck lifted his glass to his lips.

"Where did he go?" she squeaked. Holly's mind whirled as she fought the urge to scream with hysterical laughter. That was the sixty-four-thousand-dollar question, now wasn't it? "Away. He went away." She chanced a peek in Buck's direction, and could see he was waiting for the rest of the story. "To, uh, a place...where he could, uh, get, you know...in touch with his, uh..." Wife? No, couldn't say that. "In touch with his...his..."

A half smile quirked Buck's mouth as he took another sip. "Yes?"

"—in touch with his...his...feminine side." There. Of course. That made sense. Didn't it? That was partially true.

Buck nearly lost his mouthful of tea. After a brief coughing attack, he stared incredulously at Holly. "His *feminine* side?"

"Yes," Holly snapped, on the defensive. "That's what I like, er, uh, you know, *love* about him."

"His feminine side." Buck looked skeptical.

"He hides it well," she said sagely. Which was true enough. He'd been hiding the feminine aspect of his life very well.

"Why do you suppose he didn't say anything to anyone before he left?"

Holly swallowed. "It, uh, it was an emergency."

His brow knitted quizzically together. "An emergency? With his feminine side?"

"Yes," she declared with a definitive nod of her head, which she hoped portrayed a certain confidence that she was nowhere near feeling. "He is on a...mission. Of...discovery. You've heard of the...the...inner child?"

Buck shrugged.

"It's the same kind of thing."

"His *inner woman?*"

"Exactly."

Buck looked at her as if she'd suddenly begun speaking Latin. "So—" he sighed and pinched his brow "—what was the telegram about?"

"Telegram?" she choked.

"The telegram he got, just before he took off."

"Oh! Of course." She laughed gaily. "*That* telegram." She was going to kill Mac.

"Well?"

"It was notifying him that it was...time." Bobbing her head solemnly, she pretended great fascination with her iced tea.

"Time? For what?"

"To, uh, you know, go get in touch."

"With who?"

"His, uh..." she stammered. Oh, man, she thought viciously, clutching her sweating glass, first she would torture Mac, and then she would kill him. "Uh, uh, his...you know, feelings. Like I explained."

"Ahh."

Angling her head, she checked to see if he was buying this excuse.

She should have known that lifting her eyes to Buck's would be a mistake. The moment her gaze tangled with his, Holly lost all track of time and space and rational thought. Lordy, he had the most beautiful, compelling, all-knowing eyes she'd ever seen on a man. The color of rich honeyed leather, they were fringed with sandy gold lashes and—at the moment—lazily hooded.

Up close like this, she nearly felt she could see the reflection of her soul. Sparks seemed to jump from his eyes to hers and travel in a crazy, electric blaze from the top of her head to the fire engine red tips of her toes.

He raised a languid brow. "And finding this feminine side is going to take...several weeks?" he asked, his eyes never wavering from hers.

"At least," she said and nodded woodenly, feeling mesmerized. If she stared into those soft brown eyes long enough, she thought dazedly, she might never return to reality. Something about his penetrating velvety gaze, made even more alluring by its curious blend of under-standing, sympathy and irreverence, had Holly's heart thundering in her ears. Tearing her eyes from his, she focused on the whitewashed gingerbread of the gazebo. "Maybe even longer," she said, deciding to hedge her bets. "You know how these things can be."

He looked blankly at her.

"He was—" she flapped her hands, groping for the

right words ''—understandably embarrassed. Didn't want to talk about such a private thing. You understand.''

''Sure.'' Buck took another long, thoughtful pull on his glass. ''I don't mean to pry.''

''Of course.'' Holly nodded. Her eyes strayed from the ornate corbels and spindles that decorated the gazebo and cautiously back to him, and she watched his Adam's apple bob as he swallowed.

Cocking his head toward her, he thoughtfully rubbed his forefinger across his chin. ''It's just that I need to know how long we have to cover for him.''

''Cover for him?''

''Here at the ranch. And his position down at Brubaker International.''

''Oh.''

''You know he's our senior vice president in charge of acquisitions.''

''Uh… Oh. Yes.'' She and Mac had never discussed his career. He'd simply disappeared every day for eight hours, while she worked on her tan by the pool.

''Chief executive officer of Brubaker International's export division.''

''Of course.''

''General manager, Brubaker Petroleum Products Company.''

''Yes.''

''And chairman of the board.''

''The board. Mmm.''

''But you knew that.'' His eyes shot to hers.

She blinked rapidly under his scrutiny. ''Oh, yes.''

''I'm sure we can live without him for a few weeks.''

''Sure.''

''Think he'll find his—'' his lips pushed his dimples out of hiding ''—feminine side by then?''

Holly returned his grin, seeming to relax a little. "I sure hope so."

"That's good."

They rocked slowly to and fro for a moment, each lost in their own jumbled thoughts. A squirrel scolded them from a nearby tree, and overhead a large white cloud obscured the hot afternoon sun for several minutes as it floated past. The shadows were beginning to grow long across the lawn, signaling the end of yet another lazy summer weekend.

Angling his chin, Buck slanted a look at Holly and studied the curve of her cheek. Amazing. She had absolutely no idea what her fiancé did for a living. Pinching his lips between his fingers, he pondered these various pieces to their puzzling relationship. All the titles he'd mentioned earlier were held by his oldest brother, Bru, with the exception of chairman of the board. That was still Big Daddy's job. Mac's only title to date was CEO of the oil refinery division. And as far as running the ranch went, that was *his* job. Mac only dabbled nowadays. A weekend cowboy of sorts.

Why wouldn't she know that? She was a smart girl.

And what was all this malarkey about Mac needing space to discover his feminine side? Buck stifled a grin. Mac cared about many things, but his feminine side was not on the list. Holly was obviously hiding something. Yes, this inner woman deal and her unquestioning acceptance of his creative job titles had merely confirmed his suspicions that something was not quite right between Holly and his brother. This knowledge left him with a curious set of mixed emotions, for now he had an all-consuming passion to get to the bottom of this mystery, and a conscience that wouldn't let him act.

"So," he said in an effort to make conversation, "how have you been enjoying your summer?"

"It's...been very nice. Relaxing." Her smile was neutral.

He swirled the ice cubes in his glass as he pondered her words. Nice. Relaxing. Hmm. He'd file that little fact away in his mind for future examination. However, this much computed: engagement to his brother was nice. Relaxing.

"That's...nice." He swallowed the urge to snort out loud. If she'd been engaged to *him*, the words nice and relaxing would no longer be in her vocabulary. Now, thrilling and passionate and—his eyes dropped to her lips—breathtaking, that would be more like it. Man, he thought, disgusted with himself. He had to get a handle on this train of thought. Shifting uneasily, he decided to change the subject. "It's been a while since you were here last."

She nodded. "Twenty years."

Nineteen actually, Buck thought, but who was counting? "That long?"

Her smile was soft. "I was seven or eight last time I saw you."

"Eight."

"You remember?"

"We were both eight. Besides, I never forget a mud pie."

Holly laughed. "We did try to eat one once, didn't we?"

"No, no," Buck said, and gave his head a solemn shake. "You guys wanted to, but I talked you all out of it."

"Yeah, right. I seem to remember you trying to tell your sister how delicious *your* grasshopper pie was." She pulled a face. "Yeech. All those dead little grasshoppers sticking out of the top, staring at us that way. No wonder Patsy freaked out when you tried to make her eat it."

"Hey, I paid the price." He sighed in mock martyrdom. "She was always such a little tattletale."

"I remember."

Pulling a foot up onto his knee, Buck leaned into the corner of the swing, suddenly lost in the wonderful memory of their shared childhood. "For some reason, I remember us riding our bikes up and down the driveway for hours with Mac and Bru and Patsy. But I can't remember why."

Eyes drifting closed, a smile stole across Holly's face as she remembered. "We were playing wagon train. You and Mac and Bru and I made up the wagon train and poor Patsy was always the outlaw that you boys would shoot those little rubber bands at while you tried to run her off the road." Giggling, she looked guilelessly over at him and pointed an accusatory finger. "You guys were always pretty mean to her."

Buck feigned wounded feelings. "Oh, come on. She got her licks in whenever Big Daddy was around. She's his little princess, you know. We all suffered over that. Still do."

"Yeah, right. Well, how come I remember every time we played "Star Trek" in that willow tree—you know the one, down by the pond in that little gully in the South Section? How come you guys always made the little princess be the Klingon? You used to beam her in and out of that tree till her head was spinning and she ran blubbering home to Big Daddy." The swing rocked gently with her bubbling laughter.

A wide grin crept across his mouth. "Because she was such a pain."

Holly hooted. "No more so than me."

He loved her laugh. Something about it just made him feel good. "Nah." Chuckling, he gave his head a tiny shake. "You were cool. For a girl. Besides, you'd skinny-dip with us, and that was always interesting."

"That was a long time ago."

"Mmm-hmm." His eyes traveled slowly north from her ankles, pausing here and there along the way, and came to rest on her fiery cheeks. "A long, long time ago." Continuing their journey, his eyes found and merged with hers. "And whoever would have thought that you'd end up falling in love with my brother?"

The pink tip of her tongue darted out and touched her lower lip. "Yes," she murmured, and shrugged uneasily. "Who'd have thought?"

The swing slowly ceased its rocking motion, and time seemed to suspend as they looked into each other's eyes. Buck tried to ignore the intimacy created by this close contact. Suddenly he was aware of every point that their bodies touched. His thigh burned where hers leaned against his, and his upper arm fairly tingled from the warm feel of her bare skin. This assignment Big Daddy had issued was going to kill him.

A dizzying sense of yearning battled with a wave of guilt that settled like a rock in his stomach. Buck cringed. What the hell was he thinking? She was his brother's woman. And as much as she may need his help, he was beginning to need her more. And in a completely different way.

This was wrong.

No way could he do this. He had to get out of here while he still had a shred of self-respect. Tomorrow he would tell Big Daddy to find another stoolie for this project. He was far too vulnerable to Holly and her many charms to spend any length of time in her presence. He couldn't be held accountable for what might happen if he didn't nip it in the bud now.

So what if Mac had saved his life? He'd pay him back another time. Yeah, he thought, feeling decisive. The smart thing would be to steer clear. Especially the way she was looking at him right now, with those large clear hazel eyes that defied description.

Bracing his hands on his thighs, he prepared to escape while he still had two rational brain cells to rub together. "I should probably head back to the house. It's getting late." He made a production of looking at his watch as he stood and stretched and tried to seem offhand. "I...just wanted...to, you know, see how you were doing."

"That was nice." Holly picked her glass up off the floor and stood. "I'm fine," she reassured him with an airy wave.

"Good." Well. Fine. He had to leave. Now. Before he lost what was left of his mind. "Good night."

"I should probably be getting back, too. I'll go with you."

Buck closed his eyes so that he could roll them in disbelief. Was this some kind of a bizarre celestial test? Because if it was, he was beginning to wonder if he could possibly pass it. He was beginning to wonder if Saint Peter could pass it.

"Okay." He sighed and held out his hand. "Watch your step."

He was sure thunder and lightning crashed and flashed between their fingers as she placed her delicate hand in his and moved down the steps behind him.

Aw, man. He was a goner.

Chapter Three

Tossing the book he'd been reading—but not at all comprehending—onto the floor next to his bed, Buck lifted his head off his pillow and checked the hands of his alarm clock once again. Nearly midnight. The house was quiet. Hopefully everyone had gone to bed by now. Stuck in his room with nothing to do but stare unseeing at the book on tractor maintenance he'd found under his nightstand, he had been hiding out like some kind of blasted fugitive on the run.

After he and Holly had returned to the house from the gazebo, he'd given her a curt nod, barked a gruff goodnight and practically bolted to the safety of his room, where he'd sequestered himself for the entire evening. Rolling onto his side, he buried his head under his pillow and winced at the memory of her face, bewildered and slightly hurt, as she'd watched him tear up the stairs. But, doggone it anyway, he hadn't had a choice. And now he felt like a prisoner in his own home. Sitting up, Buck hurled his pillow across the room.

The frustrating thing was, this whole problem was his own doing. If he could simply keep his active libido under control where his brother's woman was concerned, he might have joined the rest of the family for dinner. He might have shared in the noisy, boisterous hilarity that had wafted up the stairs from the dining room for the better part of the evening. He might have filled his belly with a hot meal instead of the peppermint he'd found in his bureau.

His stomach growled in noisy protest of its neglect, and Buck glanced once again at the clock. By now it had to be safe to sneak down to the kitchen and return to the seclusion of his room with a sandwich, or a plate of Chef's leftovers. He was famished. He'd waited long enough for sustenance. Steering clear of Holly was one thing. Starving went above and beyond the call of duty.

The refrigerator beckoning, Buck slid off his bed, pushed himself to his feet and, pulling his Levi's up on his hips, zipped up his fly, leaving the top button undone. Dragging a hand through his hair to smooth it, he snagged his shirt off the end of his bed and padded in his stocking feet across the floor of his suite to the large mahogany double door. Slowly he inched it open and stepped into the hall.

Empty.

Good.

With a sigh of relief, he shrugged into his western shirt and—tails flapping—bounded down the giant staircase and headed for the kitchen.

Tiptoeing across the kitchen's expansive marble floor, Holly slowly worked her way through the velvety darkness toward the glass-and-stainless-steel refrigerator. Fingers probing, she found the end of the countertop and began to inch forward into the room. Not completely familiar with the less than hospitable Chef's domain, Holly hadn't been sure where to locate the light switch. But that was okay. It wasn't as if she wanted to attract any attention. The light in the refrigerator would be enough. Provided she arrived before she starved to death, she mused as she peered into the pitch-black and tried to discern a recognizable shape or two. Her stomach rumbled noisily.

"Shh," she whispered with a nervous laugh.

After Buck had so unceremoniously deposited her at the front door when they'd come back to the house from the gazebo, Holly had pleaded a headache to Miss Clarise and headed for her room. Really, she fumed, feeling disgruntled all over again as she remembered how Buck had so curtly dismissed her, he was always so hot and cold with her. One minute he was sweet and sympathetic, and the next she felt that he couldn't wait to ditch her. Well, that was fine with her. It would only make her vow to steer clear of his X-ray eyes that much easier.

Cautiously, Holly fumbled her way around the large granite-topped island, occasionally stubbing her toe or banging her shins on the hidden obstacles in her path.

"Owwch," she gasped under her breath, and bent to rub her knee. What the heck was that? Her fingers explored. Chrome bar stool. Mercy, that hurt. Suddenly she was mad at the entire Brubaker male population. If Mac hadn't up and taken off without so much as a backward glance, she wouldn't have had to spend the entire evening hiding out in her room to avoid the family's curious questions.

Or Buck's probing gaze.

Those curious, all-seeing eyes made her feel things on that single sultry afternoon in the gazebo that she'd never felt over an entire summer spent with his older brother. Vexed by this strange power Buck exerted over her, Holly vowed to fight it as she grabbed hold of the bar stool with fumbling hands and worked her way past. Whatever the underlying vibrations that roiled beneath the veneer of politeness meant, she only knew it wasn't good.

As long as she was covering for Mac, she had no business even wondering about the current that seemed to spark between her and Buck. Yes, for everyone's sake, she needed to stay away from Mac's brooding, intense, virile and—she stopped and took a deep breath—completely disconcerting brother.

Reaching the end of the counter, she lifted her arms out in front of her and headed in the direction she supposed the refrigerator to be, until her groping hands came in contact with something warm and hard and...human?

Recoiling, she stifled a scream of terror.

"Really" came the low masculine voice from the shadows directly in front of her. "We have to stop meeting like this."

When she could breathe again, Holly rolled her eyes.

"Buck?" she whispered, incredulously. She thrust her hands out in front of her once again, needing to make sure she wasn't having some kind of hallucination. Why did it seem that the harder she tried to avoid him, the more often she ran into him?

"In the flesh," he murmured as her fingertips explored his bare chest.

"Ahh. So I...see," she squeaked, and jerked her hands away as if she'd been burned.

His shirt was hanging open. Breathing a prayer of thanksgiving that the lights were out and he couldn't see her flaming cheeks, she took a step back. Gracious.

His low sigh resonated into the late-night hush, sending a ripple of awareness up her spine.

"What in heaven's name are you doing, standing around in the dark?" she demanded, hoping her cranky tone would convey that she hadn't in the least enjoyed running into his naked chest.

"I might ask you the same thing" came his retort. His baritone had a teasing edge. "I'm hiding from Chef. What about you?"

She could feel him take a step toward her.

"Me?" she squeaked. "I, uh, didn't know where the lights were. But I'll, uh, just go look for them, uh, now," she stammered, taking a step back, needing to get away from the emotions that swirled in her brain. "Just a second and I'll...ouuuwwwchhhh!" she wailed as, in her effort to escape, she managed to skewer her hip on the corner of the island's countertop.

"Hey, hey, take it easy." Buck's soothing voice reached her just before his hands did. Grasping her upper arm, he steered her against his body and supported her as she writhed in pain. "What'd you do?"

"My hip," she moaned, and, disregarding her vow to stay at arm's length, allowed her forehead to thud against the wall of his chest. "Aaachhhh." The involuntary sound escaped from her throat as her hipbone throbbed. Unable to speak, she simply stood clutching his shirt and wincing against his heartbeat.

"What happened? What did you do to your hip?" Tentatively he ran an exploratory hand from her waist to the hip she favored.

"No! No, don't!" she yelped, increasing her grip on his shirt and angling her hip away from his touch.

"Sorry," he whispered.

"I—" she attempted to gasp out her explanation "—

rammmmmed—ahhh—my hip into—ohhhh, the corner of the...counter.''

Buck groaned sympathetically. ''Aw, man, that's tough. I know that hurts. Should I call the doctor or something? I mean, are you bleeding?''

''Noooo.'' Holly took a deep breath and lightly touched her hip. Oh, baby. It felt as if she'd been wrestling a freight train. And lost. ''I'll be fiiine.'' Eventually, she thought, grimacing at the thought of the colorful bruise that would adorn her side in the morning. ''Just don't move, okay?'' She panted as the pain crested and began to slowly subside.

''Sure.''

Drawing her against his body, Buck held her steady and slowly rubbed and patted her back. It was silent in the kitchen except for the running of the refrigerator, the night sounds of cricket song and the occasional hoot of an owl that filtered in through the open windows. Teasing breezes billowed the curtains and carried into the room the sweet fragrances of summer. As the minutes ticked by, Holly's breathing slowly returned to normal. From where Buck's cheek rested snugly at the top of her head, Holly could feel his mouth move as he spoke.

''Better?'' he murmured.

''Mmm.'' She nodded beneath his cheek. ''A little.''

As the stabbing sensations in her hip ebbed, new tingly ones in the pit of her stomach took their place, and Holly suddenly knew without a doubt that they were courting disaster here. His arms tightened at her waist, and she could feel the tenor of their embrace changing in temperature. He stiffened, and Holly's breathing picked up speed and became shallow once again for completely different reasons.

The soothing motion of his hands slowed to a stop at

her back, and for what seemed like the span of a lifetime, they stood there in the dark locked together, wondering what would happen next. Against her better judgment, she leaned into his body, seeking, yearning, for what…she didn't know.

The shadow of his whiskers clung to her hair as he pulled his cheek from the top of her head. Nudging her head slightly back with his jaw, he brought his forehead to hers, his lips hovering ever so slightly above her own. Holly could feel his warm breath fanning her mouth.

Heart pounding, stomach tightening in anticipation, she lifted her chin a fraction and peered through the blackness for a glimpse of those eyes. Could he see what she was feeling in this light? They stood frozen in this intimate tableau, her mouth angled just beneath his, until she feared she would faint from longing. Was he going to kiss her? Did she want him to?

This was…crazy. The word was a whisper in the recesses of her fuzzy mind.

He pulled her impossibly closer for a brief moment, his nose brushing hers, his hands splayed at her back. Then, as if he suddenly realized where he was—and who he was with—Buck broke the spell with a heavy groan.

"Uh—" he inhaled deeply "—you should probably sit down."

She could feel his whispered words, gruff with some emotion she couldn't pinpoint, against her lips. "Probably," she agreed, though she was strangely disappointed for a woman who'd only moments ago renewed her vow to stay away from him. And, real or imagined, she thought she heard a note of disappointment in his reply, as well.

"Good," he breathed. Gently, he set her away from his body, and even in the darkness she could tell he was dragging a shaky fist over his face. "Uh, can you stand here for a minute while I get the light?"

"I think so." Removing her death grip from his shirt placket, she reached for, and finally located, the edge of the counter. "All set."

She felt suddenly bereft as he moved away. A moment later, Buck reached the switch and the overhead lights flared to life, temporarily blinding her. Holly blinked and swallowed as his startling image came into view. His shirt was unbuttoned, and beneath that she could see his bare chest as he strode to her side to help settle her into a seat.

"Here," he instructed, pulling a stool from beneath the giant island's countertop and patting the black leather cushion. "Sit."

Weak in the knees, she complied.

"You going to be okay?" he wondered, his tone slightly more brusque under the harsh light. He began to button his shirt.

Her eyes flitted to his and she knew he was inquiring about more than just her hip. "Yes. I'm fine," she assured him, feeling suddenly less than modestly dressed in her light summer nightie. Hunching forward, she huddled over the countertop and smiled brightly up at him. "It's all better now."

His expression was dubious as he moved to the opposite side of the island. "So." With the island safely between them, he braced himself on his hands and leaned toward her. "What brings you down here in the middle of the night, anyway?"

Sheepishly, she glanced up and smiled. "Same as you. I was feeling a little...peckish," she said with a light shrug. That was an understatement. At this point, a piece of that grasshopper pie didn't sound all that bad. "I missed dinner."

"Why?"

"I, uh, wasn't ready to, you know—" she lifted and dropped her shoulders "—face the questions yet. Mac is entitled to his privacy."

"Oh, right." A muscle jumped in his jaw. Pushing himself away from the counter, Buck moved toward the refrigerator. "I was just going to make myself a sandwich. Want one?"

"Sure," she breathed, crossing her arms over her midsection, hoping to muffle the grumblings from within.

"What kind?"

"Anything."

"What do you want on it?"

"Everything."

His brow quirked in amusement. "A woman after my own heart."

It was ridiculous how those simple words pleased her.

As Buck set to work, Holly tucked her hands between her knees and stared at the blurry reflection of herself in the stainless-steel appliances. The distorted image was fitting, considering she had no idea who she was anymore. And, she thought morosely, her self-image was becoming less clear by the moment. Absently, she wondered how Mac was faring, then dismissed these thoughts as abruptly as they'd come. No use worrying about him. She had enough problems of her own.

Holly allowed her eyes to stray to Buck and she watched as he prepared their food. With deft motions, he unloaded the refrigerator and cabinets of roast beef, pickles, relish, assorted dressings, bread, chips and cans of soda.

"You've done this before," she noted, observing the way he expertly sliced the meat and cheese.

"Busted." Deep dimples burrowed into the corners of his mouth, and his eyes crinkled at the edges.

Holly took this opportunity to study his face. The years had been very good to him. Buck Brubaker had grown into an incredibly handsome man. When they were children, she'd always thought him to be a cute little boy. All the oldest Brubaker boys had been, she remembered. Towheaded, with golden skin and clear, mischievous brown eyes. Johnny and Kenny had only been toddlers, and the twins, Waylon and Willie, and little Hank hadn't been born the last time she was here, so she really only remembered the oldest three, and, of course, Patsy.

Even at their tender young ages, it had been obvious that they'd all eventually tower over their father. And they had.

Yes. Buck had become a beautiful man. So rugged. So powerful. So sure of himself and his position in life. She wished she had half as much self-confidence and faith in her future at the moment.

With a flourish, Buck sliced her sandwich in two and slid her plate in front of her. "Go for it," he encouraged, noting her longing expression.

Shooting him a grateful look, Holly picked up her sandwich and, without waiting to be told twice, took a healthy bite.

"Mmm," she moaned in appreciation, her eyes closed as she chewed. "This," she mumbled, and grinned at him, "good."

Unable to help himself, Buck laughed out loud and, plopping into a chair across the island from her, went to work on his own sandwich. They ate in companionable silence, born of mutual starvation, for a while the only sounds being the clink and clank of silver against glass, and Holly's rapturous, throaty sounds of appreciation.

"This is so...excellent." She finally sighed, beginning to feel somewhat sated.

"Thanks. But you can't breathe a word about this to anyone. Chef would have my head."

Holly nodded. "Your secret is safe with me."

His dark, fathomless gaze grabbed hold of hers for a moment, as if he were trying to discern the various secrets she kept hidden in her soul. And fearful that he just may be able to discover them, her eyes flew to her hands.

"So," he asked. "What have you been up to for the past twenty years?"

"Ah," she breathed, relieved that he wasn't going to quiz her about Mac's whereabouts. She dabbed her smile with her napkin. "That's quite a bit of ground to cover. Suppose I give you the abridged version?"

Propping his elbows on the countertop, he picked his second sandwich up and held it between his hands. "If you want."

"Well, let's see. Once we moved to Oklahoma, I had to find new friends to eat mud and skinny-dip with."

Buck grinned around a mouthful of roast beef sandwich.

"After high school, my father wanted me to settle down and get married to a proper candidate of his choosing. Give him a few well-bred grandchildren."

"Sounds familiar."

"Yeah, well, if you think it's rough being one of nine children to be badgered about getting married, trying being an only child. Talk about pressure."

A glint of understanding lit his eyes.

"And I can't marry just any-old-body." Picking up her soda can, she emptied it into the glass of ice. "Ohhh, no.

George Ferguson and Big Daddy Brubaker are cut from the same cloth, I'm afraid. George is just a taller, louder, pushier version.''

"Really?" Buck stared skeptically at her. Although he didn't remember George Ferguson very well, surely nobody was pushier than Big Daddy. Setting his sandwich down, he picked up his can of soda and ran his fingertip around the rim. "Why aren't you already married, then?"

"Because—" she sighed, a devilish spark dancing in her eyes "—ten years ago my father and I declared...war. A battle of wills, so to speak. He found proper suitors, and I found ways to—" her smile was minxish as she shrugged and picked up her glass between her hands "—get rid of them. I was only seventeen when he started looking for a match that would enhance his business connections. For heaven's sake, I felt like a pawn in an arranged marriage. I had my own ideas about what to do with my life."

"What ideas?"

Holly paused, and looked up at him with a sudden vehemence in her eyes that left him breathless. Clearly she had deep feelings about the path she'd taken.

"Are you sure you want to hear this?" she asked, seeming reticent to share with someone who wasn't truly interested.

He was. "Yes. Please. Go on."

"Well." She sighed and settled against the countertop. A faraway expression crossed her face. "When I was first in college, I got a job at a halfway house for homeless children. Miracle House. Oh, Buck," she exhaled his name on a poignant breath. "I really can't describe it. It was so horrible. And so wonderful. And sometimes so...magical...that I was hooked. It was like nothing I'd ever experienced in my pampered life. And I knew from then on that I had to do something to help. To help these children who had no food," she cried plaintively. Eyes wide, she leaned toward him, her passion for her subject glowing in her expression.

"No *food,* Buck. I couldn't even believe it till I saw it with my own eyes. Some of these kids had no changes of clothing or shoes. I'd grown up with *hundreds* of shoes. Some of them were sick and had no medicine. Some had no parents, some no love...no hope." Lifting her shoulders, her eyes flashed on his. "I'd discovered my calling. I've worked for Miracle House ever since."

Brows high, Buck looked at her with a new, even higher level of respect. "I didn't know that's what you'd been doing."

"Mm-hmm. That's about the time the war began with my dad. Wanting me to get over my fascination with Miracle House, he started the son-in-law and grandchildren campaign. But at the time, marriage and family really couldn't have mattered less to me. I simply couldn't see the need to bring more children into the world when there were so many already out there who needed love and understanding and, ohhh—" she sighed sadly "—everything."

"But George doesn't understand."

"No. Don't get me wrong," she hastened to assure him. "Daddy is a wonderful man. He just wants what he thinks is best for his little girl. So, year after year, he keeps trying to find people for me to marry. Cultured people with good bloodlines, from good backgrounds with ideals that mirror his own. Unfortunately—" her eyes lit with mischief "—the blue-blooded boobs he used to set me up with have never done much for me except interfere with my goals."

"Your dad sounds a lot like mine," Buck murmured.

"Bingo." With a heartfelt sigh, Holly pushed her plate back and crossed her arms on the countertop. "I suppose I wouldn't have to listen to all Daddy's pushy advice if I moved out from under his roof, but I can't afford it. I don't make any money to speak of down at Miracle House. And, just this year, we are finally solvent enough to begin building another facility." Her eyes fairly sparkled with excitement. "We will be able to help so many more kids."

"That's fantastic," Buck said, and meant it. But at the same time, he couldn't help but wonder where Mac fit into this picture. So far, his brother hadn't mentioned any plans to move to Oklahoma. And Holly certainly didn't seem ready to give up her dreams for needy children. Well, he would try to figure that out later, when he could think straight. Right now, he would simply focus on remembering that she was spoken for. "You, uh—" he cleared his throat "—must be very excited."

"Mm-hmm. But it also means living at home, and getting along with my dad."

Buck thoughtfully stroked his chin. "Yeah, well, not for much longer, huh? I guess your folks are pretty happy about your engagement to Mac, our parents being such good friends and all."

"Oh, y-yes." Blushing furiously, Holly swallowed and attempted to explain. "Yes, they are, you know, thrilled," she admitted.

"He's got the right pedigree?" Buck's smile was sardonic.

Holly nibbled her lower lip. "I'm afraid so. My father has always liked and admired Big Daddy. So when George and Big Daddy got together and arranged for me to come down for the summer and get reacquainted with Mac, I decided in the interest of family harmony to capitulate for once. Since Miracle House has extra help from college interns in the summer, my father knew I had no viable excuse to get out of spending the summer with y'all.''

With an artless motion, Holly swept her hair out of her face and smiled resignedly. "Besides, my job can be really stressful, and I needed a break. I loved it here as a kid and found that I was actually looking forward to visiting my childhood haunts and playmates. So I packed up and headed to the Circle B.O. to meet Mac. And the rest, as they say,'' she said, suddenly studying her fingernails, "is history.''

"Love at first sight, huh?" Buck asked. His mouth went dry. Why had he asked that? He didn't want to know the answer.

"Mmm," she hummed through her bright smile. Nervously, she twisted her engagement ring around her finger. "So how about that? I was ordered like something out of the Sears and Roebuck catalog. Isn't that archaic?''

"Not when you're referring to our fathers." For reasons he could only guess to be masochistic, Buck continued to press for more information about her engagement to his brother. "Apparently you've discovered a way to keep marriage from interfering with your goals?''

Without stopping to think, Holly's answer was candid. "I really don't know." Catching herself, she backpedaled some. "I think if you are married to the right person, anything is possible. I still have so much I want to do with my life. Things that have nothing to do with the society pages.''

Leaning back into his seat, Buck laced his fingers behind his head and watched his brother's fiancée as she spoke about her dreams. She was an amazing woman. Why on earth his idiot brother would want to be away from her, in order to come to terms with his "feminine" side, was beyond him.

"Anyway, enough about me," she declared with a shake of her head. Lifting her glass to her lips, she steered the subject back to safer ground. "So tell me. Why don't you work down at Brubaker International with your two older brothers?"

"Mac didn't mention that?"

"No."

Buck shrugged easily. "Someone from the family has to keep an eye on the ranch. Until Johnny and Kenny are out of college, it's my job. Then, when they're up to speed around here, I'll take over my share of the Brubaker International responsibilities. But for now—" he leaned forward, sprawling lazily across the countertop "—running the ranch is what I do. I get a kick out of it. If Big Daddy wasn't so set on getting us all involved down at the office, I'd probably run the ranch forever. I love it."

"I can see why."

Sighing in unison, they shared a smile of understanding. Both had a passion for their work, and both had fathers who wanted them to do something else with their lives. It was uncanny how much they had in common.

Something subtle began to change between them at that moment. And as the kitchen clock ticked toward the wee hours, the conversation began to slow, becoming lethargic and a little silly. Holly's arms slid forward toward Buck on the cool granite surface of the counter and she rested her chin on her hands and smiled sleepily up at him. Her full stomach, and the pleasant conversation, had her feeling lazy and content for the first time since Mac had rocked her world that afternoon.

Impishly, she asked him if he'd seen a weather report,

and remembering his brusque behavior that afternoon, he had the decency to look embarrassed. She commented on the cricket song, and he opined that they sounded delicious. She laughed, and he chuckled. And now and then during this lazy exchange of memories and flirtations, his eyes would tangle with hers, and she would become lost for a moment in the soft, brown haze.

It was Big Daddy's voice, booming from the shadows that startled them from their trance.

"What in tarnation is goin' on down here?"

They both reared guiltily away from where they'd been sprawling across the countertop toward each other.

"Oh," the old man grunted. Clad in red-and-white striped pajamas, with a matching tasseled cap, he squinted into the bright kitchen at them, and waved a relieved hand. "It's just you two. I thought it might be an intruder. Never mind." Turning, he shuffled back into the hallway.

"I'm sorry we disturbed you, sir." Holly called after him. Her voice halted his progress. "I missed dinner tonight and found Buck down here, making sandwiches."

"That's okay, little honey lamb." Big Daddy paused and smiled pointedly over his shoulder at Buck. "I'm glad you have a little company. That's just what the doctor...ordered."

He began to leave again, but stopped himself. Leaning on the doorframe, he about-faced and addressed them both. "Oh. Speakin' of company. I've invited Bru and his wife, Penelope, to have dinner with us here at the house tomorrow night. Told them that you two would be looking forward to spendin' some time with them. So I'll expect to see you both down at the supper table?" His tone brooked no argument.

Avoiding eye contact, they both nodded.

"And, Holly honey, please accept my apologies for Mac's sudden, er, uh, sabbatical. He'll be back, quick as a rabbit, I know. In the meantime, it would mean the world to me if you would stay on, as planned, and allow Buck the privilege of squiring you around in his brother's absence. I know he's lookin' forward to gettin' to know you a little better."

Buck's smile was strained.

Big Daddy rubbed his hands together in happy anticipation. "The little missus and I are looking forward to your parents' visit."

Holly's smile was strained.

"You're part of the family now, child. Miss Clarise and I want you to make yourself at home."

"Yes, sir," Holly said with a nod, and stifled a groan. She was definitely going to commit homicide when Mac got back. How, she wondered dismally, was she supposed to give wide berth to Buck, if they were going to constantly be thrown together?

"And, son—" Big Daddy's hawklike gaze zeroed in on Buck "—I know I'm telling Miss Holly the truth when I tell her how much you want to spend a little time with her. Considering everything your brother's done for you, it's the very least you can do."

"Yes, sir," Buck said with a nod, and stifled a groan. He was definitely going to murder Mac when he got back. How, he wondered dismally, was he supposed to give wide berth to Holly, if they were going to constantly be thrown together?

Chapter Four

"**He** *what?*"

The following evening at dinner, Bru Brubaker—the eldest Brubaker son—stared across the dining room table at his brother in shocked disbelief.

Buck shifted uncomfortably in his chair. He hadn't wanted the subject of Mac's defection to come up for general discussion. Now, thanks to Bru staring agog, the entire family had their antennae tuned to their end of the table. Buck didn't even have to look at Holly, who was seated next to him, to know that she was mortified.

Without stopping to think, Buck reached down, pulled Holly's hand to his thigh and gave it a reassuring squeeze beneath the white linen tablecloth. Her fingers twined into his in a fit so natural that a fierce wave of possessiveness nearly consumed him. Swallowing past the sudden dry lump in his throat, he shot a narrow look at his oldest brother, and attempted to quell the curiosity that was directed at them by the half dozen or so family members at the other end of the table.

"It's no big deal. Apparently Mac had some...immediate...and rather private...business to look into...and he will be away for a while," Buck announced to the entire group.

Silent stares greeted this remark.

"Simple as that," Buck said with finality.

More silence.

"He'll be back." He gave his head a decisive nod. "Eventually."

More stares.

Exasperated, he rolled his eyes and pointed at the sideboard. "Hey, is that pecan pie for dessert?" He tossed this diversionary tactic out as a last resort.

The ensuing chaos left the fascinating problem of Mac's absence in the dust. At least among the younger, pie-eating crowd.

Holly applied a subtle, grateful pressure to his fingers, and Buck squeezed her hand again before she drew it back into her own lap.

The enormous mahogany table spanned the entire length of the dining room, and even so, most seats were filled tonight, in honor of their special guests, Bru and his pregnant wife, Penelope. Big Daddy and Miss Clarise occupied one end of the table with the five younger boys, while at the other end, Buck and Holly were deliberately arranged into a cozy foursome with Penelope and Bru. Buck knew that Big Daddy was simply trying to make Holly feel included by pushing them all together this way. Trouble was, Buck thought as he loosened the constricting buttons at his collar, it made it easy to forget that Holly wasn't really his date to this little social occasion.

Angling his leg, he allowed his thigh to rest against hers. After all, he was getting a cramp. Plus, there wasn't

all that much room, he rationalized. When she didn't re-
coil, he slid his arm—in a nonchalant brother-in-law-to-
be-type manner—around the back of her chair. There was
more room that way, he told himself.

Not quite ready to let the subject of Mac's disappearance die, Buck's older brother gestured pointedly with
his fork.

"What do you mean, it's no big deal? Mac just up and
left? You don't know where? For several weeks? What
the hell is going on?" Flabbergasted, Bru's eyes flashed
from Buck to Holly. "Pardon me for being nosy, but
aren't your parents coming down to meet him pretty
soon?"

"Keep your voice down, will you?" Buck ordered,
shooting Bru a grim look. Leaning back in his chair, he
exhaled and ran his free hand over the pensive lines in
his face. "Give the guy a break, will you? Obviously he
needs a little time to get in touch with, uh—" he shot a
quick look over at Holly who gave her head a nondis-
cernible shake "—to, uh, sort a few things out."

"Sorry." The eldest Brubaker brother nodded apologetically at Holly. Still clearly concerned, he shook his
head. "It's just that it's not like Mac to up and take off
this way, especially without making arrangements down
at the office. Or telling me where I can reach him, or how
long he'll be gone. And right before his own wedding?
What could be so important that he—"

"Now, honey," Penelope interrupted, patting her
handsome husband's arm and attempting to smooth
things over. "Perhaps Mac simply needed some time to
adjust to the idea of marriage. Not everyone is as sure
about marriage as we were."

Smiling into Bru's eyes, Penelope was the very picture
of a contented wife, and at eight months' pregnant, she

exuded pure maternal bliss. Her long sandy hair was swept up into an elegant chignon, and her sky blue eyes sparkled with humor and a wisdom beyond her years.

"You were sure?" Holly asked, a wistful note in her voice as she regarded the happy couple. "How did you know?" She leaned forward on the table to better hear over the boisterous cacophony taking place at the other end of the table over the slicing of the pecan pie.

"Oh," Penelope said with a gentle smile, "I think it was obvious from the beginning. Every time our eyes met, it was if an explosion took place in the pit of my stomach."

Holly blanched. "And that's how you knew?"

Bru nodded. "Yep. Every time I looked into those sweet baby blues, I knew she was the woman for me. Nothing could have kept me away from her."

Buck stiffened. "Nothing?"

"Nothing." Bru was vehement.

Against his better judgment, Buck's eyes sought Holly's for her reaction.

Big mistake.

For the moment their gazes met, it was as if two spinning planets collided in his belly. Confusion flashing in her eyes, Holly glanced quickly away and focused on her plate. Buck, feeling as if he'd just been hit with a sickening, monumental truth, did the same.

"I'm sure it will all work out for the best," Penelope offered, casting a sympathetic look at the stricken Holly. "Isn't it lucky that Buck can step in to fill the void for a while? It will give you two a chance to get better acquainted." Shifting her gaze, she trained her smile on her brother-in-law. "I know I loved having the opportunity to meet Bru's brothers before we got married. It really helped cement my feelings of belonging."

"Belonging. Oh, yes," Holly murmured, toying with her napkin. She tried valiantly to appear collected.

"It's my goal in life to make my brothers' women feel as if they belong," Buck intoned dryly. His attempt at humor fell flat.

Holly's napkin slipped off her lap and onto the floor and, glad for the chance to escape, even momentarily, she scooted her chair back and bent to retrieve it.

"I'll get it," Buck told her.

"Oh, don't bother. I'll get it."

"No problem."

"No, really—"

Awkwardly, they ducked toward the floor, fumbling for the napkin and trying not to knock each other over in the process.

"I said I'd get it," she muttered.

"I said I don't mind," he snapped.

Their eyes locked for a brief, electric moment under the table, rendering them both senseless. And breathless. And frustrated and angry with this impossible mess. Resurfacing, flushed faced and eyes sparking with their pique, together they brought the napkin to the tabletop.

"Thank you," she gasped, without looking at him.

"No big deal."

Bru frowned, obviously trying to puzzle out the underlying vibrations in the room.

Busying herself with her coffee cup, Holly turned her head, afraid that Bru would detect more than he already had. The stress was becoming unbearable, culminating in an ache that spread from her shoulders and radiated up her neck. She longed to flee from the room and have a good cry, which was very unusual considering she never gave in to such maudlin whims.

Blessedly, Big Daddy broke the tension.

"Pecan pie, Penelope honey?" he thundered down to their end of the table. "Remember now, you're eatin' for two!"

Penelope smiled and patted her burgeoning midsection. "You're sure? Looks like I've been eating for an army."

"No way! To my way of thinkin', there's nothing prettier than an expectant mother." The older man beamed. "Why, I can't wait until Miss Holly gives me a whole passel of little tykes to spoil rotten."

Nonplussed, Holly smiled weakly, then glanced at Buck for support.

"Let's not put the cart before the horse, Big Daddy," Buck advised.

Grinding his teeth, he closed his eyes and swallowed a primal scream. The idea of Holly's children being his nieces and nephews was nearly more than he could bear. Feeling that he'd taken enough punishment for one night, he pushed back from the table and patted Holly on the knee.

"Have a nice evening, everyone. I'm hitting the hay," he unceremoniously announced.

"Oh, honey," Miss Clarise chided softly as he stood and tossed his napkin on the table, "don't you want a piece of pie? It's pecan, your favorite."

"No thanks, Mama." Striding down the length of the table, he reached around and kissed his mother on the forehead. "Uncle Buck has had enough for one day." If he didn't get out of here soon, he was going to explode.

"But...but..." Big Daddy sputtered, his face turning an indignant shade of red. "But...here, now..."

"Night, Pop," Buck called over his shoulder, and headed for the door. Not chancing a look in Holly's direction—knowing those questioning eyes could render him senseless—he made good his escape. Bounding up the stairs, he headed for his room and blew through the doors. He stripped off his shirt and covered his face with it, burying a shout of fury.

She was going to marry his brother. And she was most likely going to have his brother's children.

Nothing would ever be right in his world again, he thought dismally, trying to envision how he would endure family holidays and get-togethers in the future, bouncing Holly's children on his knee and longing for their mother. It was a sick picture. Heaving a dispirited sigh, he slogged over to his bureau mirror and looked at the tortured man who stared back. That did it. He was simply going to have to toughen up. Get used to the idea. Mac and Holly. Holly and Mac. Holly and Mac's kids.

Oh, good grief.

Bracing his hands on his bureau, he hung his head and groaned. Well, if that didn't work, he'd simply have to move.

To the Yukon.

Later that evening as she prepared for bed, Holly sat at the antique oak vanity in her suite, brushing her hair and thanking her lucky stars that she'd only seen Buck once that day and that was at dinner, surrounded by his family. She was incredibly relieved to have managed to make it through "day one" without revealing Mac's precious secret. Although having hidden out in the rose garden with a book for the better part of the day didn't really give her much opportunity to spill the beans to anyone.

Keeping Mac's secret from Buck would be her biggest challenge.

Her fingers moved to the surprisingly small black-and-blue spot on her hip. Memories of last night's encounter in the kitchen assailed her, filling her with a restlessness she couldn't explain.

Tossing her brush on the vanity, she gathered her robe and stood. She walked slowly to the large French doors that lead to her private area on the veranda, and as she opened the door to the night, sultry summer breezes caressed her face and flirted with her hair.

Buck.

Why couldn't she get him out of her mind?

Tonight at dinner, she'd sensed a tension in him. It was almost as if he couldn't wait to get out of the dining room. Away from everyone. From her.

And though this thought should make her happy—especially considering how she knew she needed to stay away from him—it didn't. Instead, a whimsical melancholy settled in the back of her mind. She'd felt as if the party had left the room when he'd walked out of the dining room that evening. The conversation lost its pizzazz when Buck was no longer there. Funny, she'd never had those feelings where Mac was concerned. Or, for that matter, *any* of the blue-blooded dandies that her father had picked for her.

Holly moved to the veranda's ornate, wrought-iron railing and leaned against it, circling a post with her arms. What was going on with her? she wondered anxiously, and pressed her flushed cheek against the cool surface of the post. Was she beginning to develop some kind of an infatuation with Mac's younger brother?

No, she thought with a stern shake of her head as she set out to convince herself that this was simply not possible. Or the least bit sensible. A bubble of laughter welled into her throat. How ridiculous. Her and Buck. Buck and her.

She stared out into the vast star-filled night sky and

pondered these new thoughts. Wouldn't that set the world on its ear? she mused, briefly entertaining the idea of a relationship with Mac's handsome brother. Filling her lungs with the fresh country air, she closed her eyes. Oh, this train of thought was ludicrous.

"Don't go there," she whispered against the post. But even as the hushed words were carried away on the breeze, she began to wonder. To think about him.

He was an amazing man, this Buck Brubaker. Self-assured and strong, but sensitive, too. He'd been very understanding about Mac's absence. Not to mention supportive. And—this much she knew from observing him over these summer months—he was wonderful with horses, animals of all kinds, really, and young children, too. His youngest brother, Hank, practically idolized him, following him around, pelting him with endless, childlike questions about running a ranch. Buck was always so patient and understanding.

Then, of course, there was the matter of his eyes. Those velvety brown eyes that could read her mind and see straight into her very essence. It didn't hurt matters, either, she thought with a sigh, that he was just about as handsome as they come. Out of the three incredibly good-looking older Brubaker brothers, Buck was by far the best looking, to Holly's way of thinking.

Although, what good this way of thinking was doing her was a matter of debate.

She could never really have a relationship with Buck. Not really. First of all, whether she liked it or not, she was still engaged to Mac. At least as far as the entire family was concerned. Flirting with Mac's younger brother was definitely taboo. *At least until Mac returned and set the record straight*, a little voice in the back of her mind pointed out.

But then there was the matter of her work at Miracle House. The homeless shelter had always been uppermost in her heart and mind. Realistically, a relationship would never fit into that picture. After all, Buck lived in Texas and she lived in Oklahoma.

No. Better to simply stick to the master plan. What was that again? she wondered as she shuffled back inside her suite. Oh, yes. Break up with Mac, have a broken heart, go back to Miracle House to hide from the cruel world. She smiled ruefully as she removed her robe and slipped into bed. Somehow, the plan had lost some of its luster.

"How you doing this morning?" Buck's voice, still slightly scratchy with sleep, had Holly's stomach in a sudden tangle of knots.

After a restless night, Holly had climbed out of bed, slipped on a pair of shorts and a top and come down to the front porch to watch the sun rise and try to puzzle out a new game plan for her disgusting excuse for a life. Sitting on the top step, she slowly twisted around to find Buck leaning in the shadows of the mansion's impressive leaded-glass-and-imported-mahogany doorway. She felt as if her breath was cut off at the sight of him standing there clad in a white cotton T-shirt and a pair of faded blue jeans. He had no right to look so appealing, with his tousled hair and unshaven jaw. The blanket prints were still embedded in his cheek for heaven's sake.

She touched her lower lip with the tip of her tongue. "Fine." Her shrug was noncommittal.

"It was kind of rough, huh?" he asked, and she knew instinctively that he was referring to the questioning stares she got at last night's dinner party. Pushing off the doorway, he ambled over to where she sat on the top step and settled his lanky frame down next to her. He propped his elbows on his knees and let his wrists dangle.

"A little." Clasping her hands together, she looped her arms over her bent legs and leaned back. "I think it's kind of awkward for everyone, without Mac."

"Yeah. I know. How did the rest of the evening go?"

"You mean after you defected?" she teased.

"Yep." His smile was rueful as he cast his dark brown eyes to his fidgeting hands.

"Oh, we ate some dessert, and everyone tried to act as if nothing was amiss. You should have stayed."

Buck gave a derisive hoot. "I take it you didn't tell them about Mac's quest for his inner woman."

"Ah, no." She giggled.

Cocking his head toward her, he asked, "With Mac gone for the next few weeks, what are your plans?"

Tossing her head, she pushed her hair out of her eyes and frowned thoughtfully.

"Good question. Your father expects me to stay. And," she hastened to add, "of course, so does Mac. And then there is the little matter of my parents' visit in a few weeks. So—" lifting a delicate shoulder, Holly shook her head "—I'm staying put, I guess. But without Mac, I don't really know what I'm going to do to keep myself occupied during the evenings and weekends. Keeping me entertained was his department."

"Well, that's my job now."

Lifting a dismissive hand, she fluttered it at him. "Oh, you don't have to do that."

He snorted. "Oh, yes, I do." Jaw firm, he squinted off into the slowly rising sun.

"Oh, no. Really, Buck. I—"

Cutting her off, his eyes drifted to her profile. "It's gonna be a scorcher today. How would you feel about a swim, before everyone else gets up? We could go to the old swimming hole, for old times' sake.''

She tugged her lower lip between her teeth. No. She should simply say no. But the idea was incredibly tempting for a number of reasons. Avoiding the curious and sympathetic eyes of his family being at the top of the list, not to mention the fact that she had absolutely nothing planned to fill the yawning chasm of this day. Another dreary day spent hiding out in the rose garden certainly held no appeal. Then, of course, she thought, ignoring the worries that niggled the back of her mind, there was the glorious feeling of being alive that came from simply spending time with her old friend, Buck.

''You want to go right now?''

''Why not?''

''Don't you have work to do?''

''That's what ranch hands are for. Besides, most of my work is done. What's not done, I'll get to another day. Come on. I don't know about you, but I could use a nice...cold swim. It'll be refreshing.'' Extending his hand, he drew her along with him as he rose to his feet.

She glanced down at her small hand, linked with his larger one. Rational or not, she couldn't think of another thing on this earth that she would rather do than go down to the old swimming hole with her old buddy Buck. After all, that's what they were. Simply old buddies.

''Okay.'' She brushed past her old buddy; her breathing quickened and her stomach rolled like a tumbleweed in a hot wind. Oh, this was a mistake. ''I'll, uh, just go get my suit.''

''Whatever.'' There was a teasing light in his eye.

She paused and squinted at him. ''You're wearing a suit, too, I hope.''

"If you insist. Although, I must say, you've gotten kinda prissy in your old age."

"Oh, yeah?" Holly planted her hands on her hips and pursed her lips. "Just keep it up, mister, and you're going to be the Klingon down in the old "Star Trek" tree."

"Hmm..." he hummed. "Sounds much more interesting than it used to."

With an amused wave of her hand, Holly turned on her heel and moved to the door. "I'll only be a minute."

"Take your time. I'll get a thermos of coffee. Meet me at the barn when you're ready. We can ride down together on my horse."

"No, no, no, no, no!" Holly shrieked with laughter. "I can't!"

"Just let go!"

"Nooooo!"

"I swear, I'll catch you!"

"You used to say that all the time," she shouted gleefully, "and you never did!"

Grinning, Buck shook his head, causing a spray of water to rain in all directions. From where he stood, chest deep in the old swimming hole, he watched Holly swing out over his head on the rope that still—after all these years—hung from a branch in the old oak tree.

Her feet rested securely on the giant frayed knot, and like Tarzan's Jane, she clung to the rope—as she swung back and forth between land and water—and yodeled. "Ahh-ahhhh-ahhhhh!"

Laughing, Buck shouted up at her. "Me think Jane big chicken."

Angling her head, she stuck her tongue out at him. "Me think Tarzan big mouth."

As she soared over his head, Buck skimmed his arm

across the surface of the water, flinging a wave in her direction.

"Ahhh!" she shrieked, and giggled when the water hit its mark. "You're going to get it now!"

"Yeah, yeah, yeah. Promises, promises," he taunted, moving away from her flight path and toward the center of the pond.

The sun had moved above the horizon now, casting an already sultry heat into the little gully where they were playing, just as they had when they were children. Surrounded by leafy trees, this little world was a private oasis, grassy and cool and secluded. It was the perfect place for both children and adults to escape and play. The pond was really nothing more than a wide spot in a healthy stream that ran through the Brubaker property. And the water, so clear you could see the rocks at the bottom, was always the right temperature for a swim.

Memories came flooding back to Buck as he lazily treaded water and watched Holly's silly antics. It was amazing how nothing had changed.

And how everything had changed.

A small smile played at the corners of his mouth. Holly was wearing a suit this time. He swallowed, and passed a hand over his face. Man. Funny how he found the two-piece suit she wore infinitely more fascinating than an entire summer of skinny-dipping when they were little kids.

She was all woman now. Soft, yet firm in all the right places. Curves here, planes there and legs… He groaned. Legs that seemed to go on forever.

"Ahh-ahhhh-ahhhhh!" Holly warbled. Playfully, she pretended to beat her chest. "Hey, Tarzan!"

"Who me?" Backing up, Buck squinted at her and frowned. Something was different. Something about the rope. It was lower than it had been a few minutes ago. Not surprising, since Big Daddy had hung that rope more than two decades ago. Concerned, he moved back to the center of the pond. "Hey, Jane, I think you'd better jump."

"Why? So you can pretend you're going to catch me and then miss?" Her throaty laughter rang out over the water.

"Give me a break. That was years ago. Come on, I'm serious. I think you'd better jump this next time."

"Ha!" she shouted defiantly, and swung back out over the land. "No way."

"Holly! The rope is probably too old. Or, maybe it's the branch. Whatever, when you get out here…let go! I'll catch you, I promise."

"Oh, sure." She giggled as she soared back toward him.

A loud crack, like the report of a gun, sounded, and the rope dipped low as Holly swung past the crest and began to head back toward the shore. Screaming, she clung to the rope, and looked back at Buck with wild eyes.

"Hang on," he shouted, his heart pounding. Oh, Lord, he prayed, clenching his fists, just don't let that branch break while she's over land. "You're all right. Just be still and—"

Reaching the shore, she swung out over the rocks and started back toward him.

"—when you get out here this time, let go!"

Doing as he'd instructed, Holly waited until she reached the deep section of the pond where he stood waiting to catch her, and let go of the rope. And not a moment too soon. With a creaking groan, the old, time-weary branch snapped and gave way, falling to the water along with Holly.

"I've got you! I've got you!" he chanted, and, tensing, moved into position. "I've got you!" he shouted with confidence. He held his arms out and...missed her. He did, however, manage to catch an armload of oak leaves.

Oh, no. Where was she? he wondered, panic gripping his belly. The leaves from the fallen branch were so thick he couldn't see a thing.

"Holly!" he shouted, thrashing through the foliage, searching for her. His heart threatened to leap out of his throat. If anything happened to her, he didn't know what he'd do. "Holly!" Pushing his way through the leafy obstacle course, he frantically called her name. "Holly! For the love of Mike, answer me!"

"Way to go, you...you...big boob!" came the sputtering cry. Her head poked through the greenery as she flailed. "You said you'd catch me!"

"I tried," he growled, fighting his way through the branches and coming to her side. Gripping her around the waist, he tugged her out from under the branch and, hauling her up against his body, held her tight. "You scared the life out of me."

"You were scared?" she cried, rearing back and whapping him on the arm. "'Oh, Holly, jump,'" she mimicked him. "'I've got ya! I've got ya!' Some things never change," she griped, swiping her eyes with her hands.

Leaning back, he let loose the deep, heady laughter of relief.

"It's not funny," she grumbled, peering up at him.

"Oh, come on. You're just mad because, when we were kids, I always wanted to catch you but couldn't. The spirit was willing. The flesh was just...too skinny."

She giggled in spite of herself. "Yeah, well, that's certainly not your problem now. What's the use of having all these rippling muscles," she taunted, running her fingertips over his chest, "if you can't even catch me?"

"Oh, sure. I'm supposed to catch you, and a hundred-year-old tree. That's really fair."

They laughed together.

Pushing her wet hair back away from her face, she studied him as he held her. "Buck?"

"Hmm?"

"Why did you always want to catch me, when we were little?" Wrapping an arm around his neck, she secured herself above the water and angled his chin with her free hand so that she could see into his eyes. And what she saw there stole her breath. A yearning—so intense it hurt—reflected her own feelings. The rhythm of his breathing changed and became as heavy as her own, and as her hand slid to his chest, his heartbeat thundered beneath her fingertips. His arms circled her waist and held her firm.

"I don't know. You just brought out the protective streak in me." He shrugged. "Still do. I guess some things never change."

"And then again," she murmured, blinking the droplets of water from her lashes as she regarded him. "Some things change a whole lot."

His grip tightened on her waist, and she watched him do battle with some inner demon she was beginning to recognize in herself. Entwined this way, they studied each other's eyes, while the morning sun rose higher in the sky. Off in the distance, the sounds of lowing cattle reached them, but did not penetrate their muddled thoughts. She reached to smooth his hair. He balanced his forehead against her chin and shuddered a tortured sigh. No words were said, no promises made, but during that silent moment, the link that bound their past to their future was formed.

"We should be getting back," she whispered into the damp locks of his thick, sandy hair.

"Mmm." He closed his eyes, and a muscle jumped convulsively at his jawline.

They lapsed back into the melancholy silence of bittersweet parting, of leaving their carefree childhood and facing the complex web of their future.

Then, as naturally as if they'd rehearsed it, he turned and she slid onto his back. Locked together this way, he carried her through the water to shore. They found their clothes, put them on and collected the empty thermos and other supplies they'd brought.

Gathering his horse's reins, Buck swung easily into the saddle and held a hand down to Holly. "Let's go," he said, his dark gaze hidden beneath the broad brim of his hat. Easily, he lifted her into the saddle in front of him, and once again slipped his arms around her waist.

Holly was beginning to feel as if this were the most natural place on earth for her to be as she eased back against the firm wall of his body.

Unfortunately, given the circumstances, it was probably the most unnatural place for her to be. With a heartfelt sigh, she tentatively leaned into his embrace, swallowed the lump in her throat and tried to remember why she needed to stay away from this man.

Chapter Five

"I'm sorry. I hope you don't think that this was my idea."

Embarrassed and molten cheeked, Holly gestured to the ridiculous picnic basket looped over her arm. The giant wicker box was gaily covered with a red-and-white checked cloth, and sprouting from its depths were enough accoutrements to feed an army of gourmets. An imported bottle of wine, crystal stemware, crusty loaves of bread, assorted fine cheeses, expensive chocolates and an indistinguishable main course whose fragrance had even the horses salivating.

"Nah. It's okay," Buck assured her, then turned and yelled at his snickering ranch hands. "Shut the hell up, you boneheads! Go on. Get outta here." Taking off his Stetson, he brandished it menacingly at them. "Fuzzy! Red! You guys have work to do. Get to it." He turned and, shaking his head in disgust, leaned against the old parade wagon as it sat in the middle of the paddock, just outside the barn. "Sorry about that."

"No," Holly murmured. "I should be the one apologizing. I can see how busy you are." Bristling uncomfortably, she glanced around at the half dozen or so ranch hands that—when they weren't grinning at her and their boss or guffawing amongst themselves—were pretending to work. How juvenile, she fumed, feeling conspicuous. Why, they acted as if they'd never seen a picnic basket before. A glance down at her burden had her grimacing. Well, chances were they'd never seen one quite like this.

Deciding to ignore them, she trained her eyes on their boss. It had been nearly a week since she and Buck had gone swimming in the pond, and as the week had passed, a routine of sorts had begun to develop between them. Holly had done her best to avoid Buck and he had done his best to avoid her. And except for the occasional meal together—where they'd given in to furtive peeks across the table—they'd managed to stay out of each other's way. Until now.

Shifting the basket higher in her arms, she looked up at him. "I can bring this back at a more convenient time, if you like."

"Not at all. In fact I was just thinking about taking a lunch break."

"Really?" Holly lifted her shoulders and gestured to the basket she'd lugged down from the house. "Well, that's good, because your father sent you enough food to last all week. You should probably call those, er, boneheads back over here." Grinning, she inclined her head in the direction of his hands. "There's enough for everyone."

Buck's brows drew into a quizzical line. "Big Daddy sent this?" Reaching down, he lifted the portable restaurant out of her arms and eyed it skeptically.

Head bobbing, Holly nodded. "Mmm-hmm. He said

you were very superstitious about having a picnic lunch at least once a week, ever since you nearly drowned in a cow tank as a child. He said you did it to honor Mac?''

Scratching his temple, Buck simply stared at her, and flatly repeated her words. ''I do it to honor Mac.'' What was the old man up to now? he wondered with suspicion, his gut clenching.

''That's...nice,'' she commented, and looked curiously up at him, as though she didn't quite make the connection between the symbolism of his supposed culinary ritual and his being dragged out of a cow tank by Mac as a kid. ''Big Daddy said since he was too busy to deliver it himself, it would be a big help if I would bring it to you. And since I didn't have anything else all that pressing to do—'' she grew slightly flustered at his blank expression ''—I said, um, well, you know, sure. So. There you go.''

She patted the basket he now held and took an uncertain step backward. A ranch hand let loose with some raucous laughter, drawing her attention to the other end of the paddock, where six pairs of curious eyes watched their boss stare in amazement at his ''lunch.''

Buck groaned. Big Daddy was jerking his chain again. Reminding him that he owed his brother. Forcing him to spend time with Holly, against his better judgment. Obviously, he was being reprimanded for neglecting to do his chaperoning duties with her this past week. Lifting his free hand, he pinched the tightly coiled muscles in the back of his neck. Would this misery never end?

Every night, as he lay in his bed thinking of Holly, he'd tossed and turned and agonized over what to do about this unbearable situation. Last night, tortured by shame and worry over his growing attraction to her, he'd thrown back his blanket and gone outside his own glass doors to stand on the veranda to stare at the sparkling night sky. And though he'd wrestled with, and thought about, and prayed over, the problem for more than half the night, no solution came to mind. No peace for his battered conscience. No balm for his weary spirit.

He'd continued to do battle with these troubling emotions this entire morning, and now here she was, tempting him all over again. With a picnic lunch, no less.

Exhaling heavily, Buck set the gargantuan picnic basket on the old wagon and turned to look at Holly as she watched his men horsing around. She certainly didn't seem to be all that fazed by Mac's disappearance. Or if she was, she was handling it amazingly well. She was so stoic. So strong. Filled with such an inner peace and calm. What a woman she was, he thought admiringly.

As Buck watched her standing there in the dappled shadow of a leafy tree—a serene smile resting lightly at the corners of her sweet mouth—he somehow began to feel a little sense of calm acceptance steal into his weary heart. It was almost as if he was starting to realize that there was nothing he could do about this mess. Nothing. He couldn't escape and neither could she. Buck rubbed his jaw as this new thought suddenly struck him.

It would run its natural course, whether he liked or not. So, he figured, he could spend the next few weeks wallowing in misery, or he could change his attitude and try to enjoy what little time he had left with her. For soon, Holly would be a married woman, and she and his brother would find a place of their own.

Thoughts of Mac drifted into the mix. Yeah. Somebody should be enjoying Holly's company. It was clear his brother wasn't too concerned about spending time with her. He still couldn't get over the bitter feeling that if Mac really cared, he'd be here with this woman.

A tired sigh shuddered through his body. He felt as if he were far older than his twenty-seven years. The age-old phrase "If you can't beat 'em, join 'em" echoed in his mind, and it was then and there that he decided to quit fighting for a little while. At least long enough to eat the lunch she'd so thoughtfully lugged all the way down here from the house. He'd work on his noble efforts to steer clear of her later. When he wasn't quite so hungry.

"Would you care to join me for lunch?" he suddenly heard himself asking.

"Me?" Holly's eyes darted from the ranch hands she'd been watching with interest to Buck.

"As you say, there's plenty of food." He rolled his eyes. "Part of my superstition, I guess. Anyway, I'd be pleased if you'd stay."

Vacillating for a moment, her eyes darted from the basket to him and back to the basket. "It does smell really good in there," she admitted.

"Yeah, well, out here it stinks." He looked pointedly at his gawking ranch hands. "Let's go somewhere a little more pleasant than this."

Holly grinned. "Okay. You lead. I'll follow."

Hoisting the picnic basket out of the wagon and into his arms, Buck simply nodded.

"Uggh." Holly leaned back against the tree and patted her stomach. "I'm stuffed."

So far, they'd sampled nearly everything in the basket, and were basking in the afterglow of a sumptuous repast. The company had been more comfortable than either had imagined, given the strain they each privately harbored toward their blossoming relationship as adults. They'd spent nearly as much time talking and laughing as they had eating, and now, as their lengthy lunch hour came to an end, they were reticent to go back to the real world.

"Me, too. I need a nap now." Closing his eyes, Buck crossed his arms behind his neck. The red-and-white tablecloth made a remarkably comfortable resting spot, as it lay spread out on a patch of grass beneath a small grove of trees behind the stable. Sprawled out next to Holly, he exhaled in satisfaction and began to relax for the first time in months. He could lay here like this for the rest of his life, he decided, feeling uncommonly happy and content.

His nose itched. Languidly he reached up to rub it, and discovered a blade of grass hovering above his face. Opening his eyes, Holly's minxish grin came into focus, the long stalk of grass dangling from her fingertips. Before she could react, his hand shot up and caught hers. "Gotcha." His mouth playfully mirrored her grin.

"You can't go to sleep on me," she scolded, a mild complaint in her voice as she leaned toward him.

"Why not?" he murmured, feeling incredibly lazy. His hand moved over hers and their fingers laced easily together.

"Because we still have more eating to do."

"Get outta here," he moaned.

Rummaging around in the depth of the basket with her free hand, she came up with an elaborately foil-wrapped chocolate and waved it under his nose. "Come on. You want a chocolate. You know you do."

"You are an evil temptress," he teased, and rolled over on his side to face her. His expression sobered as the meaning of his words struck him.

"Sorry." She looked truly contrite, and for a moment they sat looking at each other, silently acknowledging that something was going on between them. Something they couldn't speak of. Or act on. Something with which they each had to cope. There was some comfort in that.

"Don't be," he said.

Extracting her fingers from his, Holly cleared her throat. "It's awfully thoughtful of you to do this." She gestured to the remnants of their lunch. "In Mac's honor and all. Thank you for inviting me."

A flash fire of guilt roared through his belly. "Mac is a great guy."

"Yes." Holly nodded. "He is."

"I owe him a lot."

"Yes. Me, too," she agreed.

With a groan, Buck rolled over on his back and stared unseeing at the expansive blue sky that seemed to go on forever overhead, and fought his feelings of hopeless longing. What was happening here was forbidden. Sooner or later, he would get that through his head.

Time to change the subject, he decided, and with a brusque shake of his head he propped himself up on his elbow and peered up into her adorable face.

"So where are you planning to set up this second branch of Miracle House?" he asked offhandedly.

Her expression softened, and a small, satisfied smile tipped her mouth. "We haven't gotten that far in the planning stages yet. Could be anywhere, I guess." Eyes glowing, she sat forward and regarded him, an excited quality creeping into her voice. "I'd love to see the new location somewhere out of the city limits, though. I've always dreamed of someday purchasing some acreage, a farm or something like that. It would be a chance for some of these kids who've never been out of the city to get back to nature. You know, to get completely away from the environment that has been so hurtful to them and give them a peaceful place to heal, and find happiness and health.''

"Kind of like the way we grew up? A big old ranch house, lots of space to roam, maybe a few horses to ride?''

"Yes,'' she enthused, clasping her hands in rapture at the image he painted. "A few bicycles, a pond for swimming and some trees to climb. Lots of love and laughter. Just like our childhood.''

"Sounds great,'' Buck agreed, smiling at her eager expression. "I know that there are some pretty successful dude ranches and camps of that nature that cater to needy kids. It couldn't be too tough to set up something like that as an offshoot of Miracle House,'' he said, the wheels in his head turning in rhythm with hers. "I'd bet it could be very rewarding, running such a camp,'' he mused. "Sounds like a lot of fun. You're lucky.''

"Oh, I don't know,'' she responded, leaning forward and hugging her knees to her chest. "There would be a lot of rough edges to work out first. Finding the right piece of property, and the right people to run the place. I think the people I work with would be very interested in heading in that direction, if I could put a decent business plan together.''

"Well, that shouldn't be too much trouble. We Brubakers know all about running ranches, and putting business plans into action, so you've come to the right place for ideas.'' He grinned at the irony. "I could help you put something together that might get you on the right track, if you want.'' Heck, he thought, warming to the idea, he could run a little operation like that with one arm tied behind his back.

"That would be great!'' Holly exclaimed, really beginning to get into the idea. "I'd really love that.''

"Me, too." Boy howdy, so would he. Spending time planning her dream with her, then helping her bring it to fruition, would be one of the most exhilarating experiences of his life. But, his nagging conscience reminded him, helping her plan her dreams was the job of her future husband. Stoically, he forced himself to add, "Mac will probably be able to give you a lot of insight on your idea, too. He's a real whiz at business."

Her smile faded, ever so slightly. "That's true."

Glancing at his watch, Buck started. "Uh-oh. I gotta go. I've been gone far too long. I'll never hear the end of this from the guys."

"Oh! Of course."

Inclining his head toward her, his dimples bracketed his mouth. "Thanks for joining me for…this, uh, lunch." He pointed sardonically at Big Daddy's flamboyant care package. "I'm really glad that you could stay and help me with it."

"Me, too." Her eyes flashed to his, telling him that she meant it.

"Need any help hauling this monster back to the house? I could always throw it into the back of my truck and haul it back for you."

Holly giggled. "No. It's a lot lighter now. Thanks, though."

"Sure." Pushing himself to his feet, he extended a hand to her. "See you later?"

"Yes." Standing, she faced him and, after vacillating for a moment, touched his elbow. "Buck, I—" she hesitated as she carefully picked her words "—I wish you wouldn't feel obligated to entertain me. Just because Mac's gone."

"I don't."

"You're sure Big Daddy isn't pushing you to spend time with me because he feels sorry for me?"

The muscles jumped in Buck's jaw as he pondered his response. "I always end up doing exactly what I want to do. Regardless of what my father may say or do."

"Really?" she whispered, a light of pleasure flickering in her uncertain eyes.

"Yep." He sighed, calling himself every kind of fool as the truth of that statement hit home. "Really."

And so the moratorium ended. Finally bowing to Big Daddy's incessant demands, Buck decided it would make fewer waves to simply stop avoiding Holly, and give in to the pure pleasure of her company. To pacify Big Daddy, if nothing else. Besides, finding new and creative ways to steer clear of her was becoming downright impossible, living as they did under the same roof.

Once Buck had accepted his lot as Holly's chaperone, the rest of the following week was spent in relatively easy camaraderie. As easy as his troubled mind could be, given the circumstances.

Not trusting himself to spend idle time alone with Holly, Buck filled the days with exhausting activities. Horseback rides into the thousands of acres that made up Big Daddy's expansive property, impromptu swim parties in the Brubakers' Olympic-size outdoor pool, lunches on the veranda, brunches in the rose garden, munchies in the gigantic home theater, and all of this with a younger brother or two in tow.

For his sanity's sake.

Because every fiber of Buck's being cried out to be alone with Holly. He longed to take her in his arms, kiss her senseless and beg her not to marry his thoughtless and unfeeling brother. But he would never allow himself to do something so reprehensible. Even if he did suspect that her relationship with Mac wasn't all it was cracked up to be. Even if he knew that he was the man she should be marrying, and not his brother.

So, though it was slowly killing him, Buck did his best to grit his teeth and remain as politely aloof as he could where she was concerned. It was a hellish test of character.

Especially considering the fact that Holly was such a free spirit at heart, always laughing, teasing and drawing him irrevocably closer. She was one of those people who thought nothing of looping her arm through his, or touching his jaw, straightening his hair, or lightly patting his back. It was enough to drive a lesser man to distraction. At times, Buck couldn't help but wonder why she didn't seem the least bit conscious of the effect she was having on him. Perhaps because she did not feel for him what he felt for her.

But there was something there. He'd seen it in her eyes.

And still there was no word from Mac.

This emergency leave had gone on for more than two weeks now, and aside from the occasional reassuring mention from some member of the family or another that "Mac will surely be showing up at any minute," he was largely not only out of sight, but out of everyone's mind, as well. So they continued to bide their time the best they could until the return of the prodigal son.

Having exhausted every conceivable entertainment available here at the Circle B.O., Buck dug two old bicycles out of the barn and—in a fit of nostalgia—invited Holly for a ride up and down the driveway. Alone. For old time's sake. After all, he rationalized, there were only two of their old bikes left after all these years. Certainly

they could spend one lazy Thursday morning alone together, wobbling down the driveway on rusty bicycles
and reverting to their childhood.

And he'd been right about one thing. Holly loved the
idea.

Though the sun was beginning to blaze overhead, it
was cool in the long tunnel created by the shade trees
that lined the mile-long driveway. Feeling carefree and
giddy as a truant schoolgirl, Holly giggled as she struggled to keep up with Buck. Why had she agreed to do
this again? She peeked at his broad back as he rode just
ahead of her, and was suddenly reminded. Everything
was wildly fun if Buck was involved. Heck, she thought,
still giggling as she labored, she'd have walked down the
driveway on her hands if he'd suggested it.

"How come this bucket of bolts is getting so hard to
peddle?" she huffed, and stood for better leverage. Her
tire was emitting a most suspicious high-pitched whining
sound.

Tucking his chin into his shoulder, Buck peered over
his shoulder at her tire. "Looks like you've got a flat."

"Oh, great, you give me the loser bike and you get
the cool banana bike," she groused good-naturedly, finally grinding to a stop. "Hey, wait up," she shouted,
"I can't do this anymore. Trade me." Extracting her legs
from her dented and rusty bicycle, she propped it against
one of the many shade trees that lined the driveway and,
planting her hands on her hips, narrowed her eyes at him.
"After all, this was your idea."

Buck snorted. "Yeah, right. Like I'm going to give
you the cool banana bike, and ride that piece of junk bike
with a flat tire. No way." Laughing, he turned around
and slowly began to circle her. "But," he said, lifting a

teasing brow, "if you are a very good little girl, I'll let you ride on my handle bars."

Her hoot of laughter shot skyward and jolts of delight jumped between her shoulder blades. Though she found his dimpled smile completely irresistible, and longed to throw her arms around his neck and ruffle his thick, sandy hair, she clasped her hands together and tried vainly to resist his charm.

"I am having total déjà vu." Pretending to pout, she angled her head toward him. "You used to say that same baloney all the time as a kid, and I have the scar over my right eye to prove it." Holding her arms out, she flexed her muscles and parroted his youthful boastings. "'Come on, Holly, you can ride on my handle bars. I won't let you fall.'"

"Will you ever give me a break about that?" he grumbled.

"No."

"Get over here, woman," he ordered, peddling toward her, his knees at right angles, his front wheel careering to and fro.

"No way," she cried, giggling as he braked to a stop and, reaching out, grasped her wrist to steady himself. "Buck, no. I didn't think this was a good idea when I was a kid, and I still don't." Her protest was largely ignored as he tugged her to his side, but Holly didn't care. The mirth welled in her throat as she looked at him and suddenly saw the little boy with whom she spent her childhood days playing. He was just as cute now as he was then, the same boyish light in his eyes, the same vulnerable expression on his face. But there was a maturity there now that hadn't been there before. A gentleness. And an attraction.

Her heart rolled over, and she suddenly realized just

how deep her feelings for this man ran. The sparks of friendship that had begun a lifetime ago were now flaring to life in a deeper, more meaningful way. Wouldn't her father fall into an apoplectic fit when he realized he'd hooked her up with the wrong Brubaker? Holly pushed the niggling worry to the back of her mind. They would deal with that unpleasantness another day.

"I'm tellin' ya—" he chuckled "—that's why I grew all these muscles."

Involuntarily, her eyes flitted over his rugged build. "Oh, is that why?" Sliding her hand up his arm, she playfully squeezed his steely bicep. "Just so you could ride me on your bike."

"Among other things. But those are other activities for another day."

"You and your activities," she mumbled. Much to her annoyance, her cheeks caught fire. She didn't want him guessing about the feelings she was battling. At least, not until Mac came home.

Eyebrows arched, his dimples came out of hiding and he laughed. "Come on now," he coaxed, "this time I mean it. I won't let you fall." Before she could escape, he reached around her waist and lifted her into his arms.

"Buck!" Gasping, she squealed with laughter. "Put me down. I'm not going to ride on your handlebars," she squeaked, and gripped his broad shoulders for support. With seeming effortlessness, he settled her—facing him—onto the bent and rusted bars, and then gripped the handles, essentially locking her in place. Screeching all the while, she twined her hands around his neck and, hanging on for dear life, couldn't remember the last time she'd had quite so much fun. She'd probably been eight. "Buck!" she gasped, "No!"

"You're telling me that you would walk all the way home?" he grunted, fumbling for the pedals with his feet.

Holly peered down the endless stretch of driveway. He did have a point. "Well, no," she argued weakly, still feeling intoxicated with joy. "But c'mon, this poor thing is too old to hold both of us. You should have thrown it away years ago. It looks—" she peered around behind her at the randomly spoked wheel on which Buck was balancing her and shook with dizzy hilarity "—as if it's been thrashed by at least a dozen kids."

"It was," he agreed. His chuckle was amiable as his eyes settled on hers. "But it has sentimental value. Like a dear childhood friend."

Holly's heart leapt as their eyes tangled and danced for a moment. "I didn't know you were so sentimental," she whispered, trying to inject a teasing note into her voice, though she felt faint. There noses were mere inches apart.

"Only where you're concerned." After a supercharged eon, Buck drew a ragged breath and shook his head. "Hang on."

He didn't need to tell her twice as, with a lurching start, they were off, weaving helter-skelter down the driveway together, clutching each other and laughing as if they'd stepped two decades back in time.

When at last they reached the barn, Buck pulled to a stop and, leaning forward, gathered Holly into his arms. Holding her tight, he stepped away from the bike and nudged it out of the way with his foot. With an ease that never ceased to amaze her, he lowered her down the solid wall of his body till her feet hit the ground. Heart palpitating, she clutched the front of his shirt for support.

She tried to swallow past the wad of cotton that had become her tongue as she glanced at him and cleared her throat. "I'm, uh, just going to go get cleaned up for lunch."

His eyes twinkled into hers. "Okay. Save me a seat."

"Yes," she agreed, smiling shyly up into his handsome face, still feeling eight years old. "Thanks for the bike ride." Suddenly realizing she was clutching the front of his shirt in her fists, she released her fingers and smoothed the fabric over his chest. "Sorry."

"It's okay." He tugged a strand of her hair away from her mouth.

"I'll see you in the house."

"Mmm-hmm."

"Okay, then. Good. Thanks—" she felt as if she could stand there, gazing into those velvety brown eyes all day long "—again. You know, for the ride."

"Anytime."

His voice was low and husky and sent shivers up her spine. Unable to think of any other reason to loiter out here in the paddock, Holly turned and headed toward the house. Pausing midway, she turned and waved. He'd been watching her. She was used to that now, she thought with a dazed smile, and, gathering her skirt, dashed to the house.

"Been bike ridin', I see."

"Yep."

Big Daddy moved into the shadowed interior of the stable toward his son, a gleam of concern in his eye. "Well, that's good. But you know, boy, I asked you to keep that little gal company. Not flirt with her." The older man's chuckle boomed, but there was a warning in his tone.

"What?" Slowly and deliberately, Buck turned to stare in shock at his father. What the hell? He'd done his level best to be a complete and total gentleman when it came to this woman. What, for crying in the night, did Big Daddy expect from him?

"Just don't go turnin' her head, boy" came Big Daddy's good-natured command. Again his laughter boomed to break the tension. "Other than that, keep up the good work." With this last edict, Big Daddy waved jauntily and moseyed back into the bright afternoon sunlight.

A muscle twitched in Buck's jaw.

Not trusting himself to speak, he simply stared after his father. Then, in a blind rage, he headed to his horse's stall and decided to get some real work done. Criminy damn. He couldn't win for losing. He'd tried to stay away from Holly. But what did it get him? A raft of flack. So he finally bowed to the pressure and did his father's bidding. And what the hell did he get? he wondered as he furiously saddled his mount. A damn raft of flack.

Well, that was the straw that broke the rancher's back. He couldn't take it anymore. If his feelings were obvious to Big Daddy, then they would certainly be obvious to everyone else. Guilt, like the flames of a forest fire, licked his belly, threatening to consume him.

Gathering the reins, he lead his horse into the sunlight and swung into the saddle. Mind whirling, he knew he had to take action to solve this problem. Taking several weeks off work to entertain his brother's woman was definitely not productive. Snorting, he nudged his mount toward the open road. Yeah, he thought grimly, it was finally time to get serious about dating some other women. That would make everyone happy.

Everyone but him.

Grimacing, he decided that, for now anyway, he'd skip lunch, bury himself in some work and stay away from the house till he cooled down. As furious as he was now, that could take days. When he was feeling a little better, he'd dig out his standby list of phone numbers. A list he'd neglected since Holly had arrived. Well, no more. Joanne was always up for a good time. And he'd been meaning to give Rhonda a call, before Holly had arrived and blown those intentions out of the water.

Hitting the open road, he urged his horse to run. And as he tore across the endless expanse of golden ranch land toward the far horizon, he knew to a large extent he was trying to flee from his guilt.

By the time Friday afternoon arrived, Holly was sure that Buck was avoiding her again. The fun had ended far too abruptly. But why? she wondered as she rocked despondently back and forth on the glider swing in the old Victorian gazebo. Had she said something to offend him?

She racked her brain, but came up with no clues. He hadn't shown up for lunch yesterday afternoon as he'd promised. And, that evening, he'd been noticeably absent from the dinner table. When they'd passed in the hall later, he'd given her a curt nod and disappeared into his room, leaving her to spend the night wringing her hands and wondering what she'd done wrong.

Where was her buddy Buck? Her friend. Her—she tugged her lower lip between her teeth—*good* friend. In her heart of hearts, Holly knew that Buck had become more than a good friend to her. Much more. So why the cold shoulder? Were they getting too close? Was that why he'd disappeared? She stared unseeing at the formal gardens that made up the front of the mansion and sighed heavily. A loneliness that she'd never experienced before stole into the corners of her heart and left her feeling depressed. Setting the swing into a despondent motion with her foot, she leaned back in the seat and tried to swallow the growing lump in her throat.

If she could just hang on till Mac came back, everything would be all right.

An hour later, Holly found herself headed toward the illusive South Section, a woman with a dubious mission. When Big Daddy had suggested that she take this note out to Buck, she'd jumped at the idea. Perhaps this would give her the opportunity to figure out what was wrong, she'd reasoned as she smoothed her damp palms on her brightly colored shorts. But now, as she trundled over hill and dale, down the dusty road that Buck's father had assured her would lead to him, she began to have her doubts. What if he didn't want to see her? What if she was interrupting his work? What if he got mad?

What if, what if, what if?

The words spun in her head till she wanted to scream.

Lifting a hand, she shielded her eyes from the beating sun and, squinting off into the distance, felt her heart lurch. There he was. Just beyond a little grove of trees, off to the side of the road. She could see him standing next to his pickup truck, taking a drink from a canteen. Clad only in a pair of blue jeans and cowboy boots, when he'd drunk his fill, he poured the rest of what must have been water over his head and bare torso. With a shake of his head, he ran his hand through his hair and over his chest.

Mesmerized, Holly stood watching him and attempted to swallow. The man standing before her was magnificent. They'd gone swimming before, but they were in the water so much of the time, she hadn't had the opportunity to really study his impressive build. Bronzed by the summer sun, Buck leaned back against his truck, giving her a chance to inspect, undetected, the washboard stomach, the well-formed pectorals, the bulging triceps, the smooth, broad, perfectly rounded shoulders. She flexed her hands at her sides, and exhaled the breath she'd unconsciously been holding. Forcing her feet to move, she slowly approached.

He didn't notice her until she was nearly upon him, and when he turned and spotted her, a raw emotion filled his eyes that spoke to her of some kind of mental anguish. They stood staring at each other that way for endless minutes, each consumed with longing, and guilty fascination. Taking several steps, Holly came near enough to smell his after-shave and feel the damp heat radiating from his body. Her eyes darted around in confusion, and finally—finding her voice, tinny as it was, she fished the missive that Big Daddy had sent along out of her pocket.

"Your father wanted me to bring this to you."

"He did?" Buck took the note without glancing at it. His tone was gruff.

"Yes," she whispered, feeling miserable. What was wrong with him? Why was he acting so distant? "Okay, then," she said with a stoic nod as she took a step back and prepared to follow the long road back to the house. "I should be on my way."

"Holly."

"Yes?"

"Hang on just a second, will you?" He sighed. He tore open the note from Big Daddy and scanned it. A rueful smile twisted his handsome features. "It would seem that Big Daddy has organized a little barbecue party for tonight." He glanced up at her and crossed his arms at his chest. "Looks like I'm supposed to head back to the house with you and get cleaned up."

Holly's glance darted from the note he held to his face

and her stomach clenched. He looked anything but pleased. "Oh, really, don't worry about me," she chirped with false bravado in an attempt to let him off the hook yet still maintain her battered pride. "I can find my own way back."

"Don't be ridiculous. I'll take you back." His grim tone brooked no argument as he unfolded his arms and slapped the door of his rig with an open palm.

Clearing her throat, she wrapped her arms around her middle. "Buck," she began tentatively, then continued on in a rush, "I'm sorry you've had to spend so much time with me." Her voice began to falter, and her chin to quiver.

He opened his mouth to speak, but she pressed on.

"I know Big Daddy is pushing you to entertain me. He's embarrassed that Mac left me here." Tears pricked the backs of her eyes. She knew she deserved every moment of agony she was experiencing for all the lies she'd told, but that didn't make it any easier. "I know that you probably have a million things you'd rather be doing than spending all this time with me."

"Is that what you think?" His eyes glittered as he pushed off the side of his truck and took a step toward her.

She didn't respond, but instead hung her head and closed her eyes, squeezing back her silly tears.

"Holly."

Lifting her watery gaze, she looked up and stared in distress at him. His eyes had softened and concern etched his brow.

"What's wrong? Honey," he urged, reaching out and grasping her arms to draw her close, "tell me. What's wrong between you and my brother?"

"Nothing," she choked.

"Something is wrong. You can't deny it. He hasn't called once in the two weeks he's been gone, and everyone knows it." Tilting her chin, his eyes flashed into hers, and his fierce expression told her that if Mac were there, he'd probably better start running again. "Tell me," he insisted. Pulling her with him, he leaned back against the truck and tucked her next to him, against the side of his body. He draped a brotherly arm around her shoulder.

Leaning tentatively into his smooth, warm embrace, she shook her head. "I can't."

"Why not?"

"Because, I—" her voice was thready with emotion as she whispered "—I promised." Looking up, she pushed her hair away from her eyes and studied the sympathetic expression that was nearly her undoing.

"And you keep your promises." He sighed, and stroked her cheek with a gentle fingertip.

"Yes." She sighed, too, but couldn't remember why anymore.

"I admire that."

She gave her head a subtle shake. She was anything but admirable. There were so many things she wanted to say, but didn't know where to begin. Desperately, she wanted to tell him the truth. To confess this entire sick joke and beg forgiveness for deceiving him and his entire family.

She froze as the idea began to crystallize in her mind. Of course. Why couldn't she do that? The truth was always the best way to go. Surely Mac couldn't have foreseen what keeping his secret would do to her. To the rest of his family. Surely he would understand if she confided in Buck, close as they were to each other. After all, he couldn't expect her to carry on this ridiculous charade by herself forever.

If she was going to do it, she decided with dogged determination as Buck cradled her shoulder in his hand, she had to do it now. Before she lost her nerve. Tears of tightly wound emotion welled into her eyes, and she took a deep breath to plunge in.

"Oh, Buck, I'm so sorry," she murmured, groping for the words. She twisted her engagement ring as she fumbled to make him understand. "I'm so very sorry... I—"

"Hey," he admonished, and angled his cheek to rest at the side of her head as they stood side by side, "don't. None of this is your fault."

"Yes," she insisted. "You don't know. I—"

"I know that my brother doesn't seem to have any respect for what a wonderful woman he has."

Holly could feel the muscles of his jaw working angrily at her temple. He thought she was wonderful? His unexpected words filled her with a curious mix of guilt and pleasure. "Oh, no, that's not true. Actually, Mac has been—"

"It *is* true." His voice was vehement as he interrupted. "He should never have left you this way. No matter what the emergency."

"No," Holly whispered, tears beginning to spill down her cheeks.

His fierce, protective words were not making this any easier, but she had to come clean now or die trying. She couldn't keep up this ruse another minute. It was all so clear now. She suddenly knew without a doubt that she loved this man. Had loved him since she was just a little girl.

Peeking up, she implored him with her water-filled gaze. "Listen to me. You can't blame your brother for leaving me this way. None of this is his fault. In fact, I was the one who—''

''Hey, hey, shh,'' he whispered. Framing her cheek with his hand, he angled her tearstained face so that he could look into her eyes. ''Oh, honey, don't cry. Stop blaming yourself.''

''But you don't understand...''

''I understand plenty,'' he gritted out, and rested his forehead against hers. ''I understand that you are an amazing, beautiful woman who needs to be loved and cared for.'' His urgent words came in a heated caress against the wisps of hair that rested against her cheek. ''I understand that he's not living up to his end of the bargain. And I understand this much. If you were mine...'' he vowed with a groan, and, pushing off the truck, pulled her to him. Bracing his arm on the cab's roof, he leaned against her. He pressed her body between his and the warm metal of the truck door. Eyes flashing, he swore, ''I'd never let you out of my sight.''

''You wouldn't?'' she breathed.

''No.''

They gazed helplessly at each other, powerless to stop the avalanche of emotion that threatened to consume them.

With a tortured sigh, Buck's mouth searched for, and found, Holly's. Like a weary soldier stumbling home after an endless battle, he cupped her face and took sustenance from her sweet, exquisite mouth, stealing her breath, her strength to fight and—most of all—her heart. Their kiss was hot, hungry and passionate and laced with forbidden dynamics that only added to the tension of the moment. Tossing the taboos that had plagued them to the sultry Texas wind, they clung to each other, eagerly exploring this new aspect of a relationship that had been budding in the secret corners of their hearts all summer long.

When Buck angled her head back and rained a trail of kisses down her neck and into the hollow of her throat, Holly thought she'd surely perish from the ecstasy. Curling her fingers into his shoulders, she nudged his head back up to her mouth where, once again, he fiercely staked his claim.

As a gentle breeze flirted with their hair, the only sounds out in the South Section were the gentle lowing of a nearby herd of cattle, the occasional song of a distant bird, their ragged breathing and the low guttural groan emanating from deep within Buck's soul.

Lacing his fingers in her hair, he angled her mouth for a deeper kiss, struggling to draw as close as humanly possible to a woman who could never belong to him. She tasted of female, fresh and sweet, delicate yet powerful, like no woman he'd ever known. He had to experience, if only this once, the thrill of her kiss. What he was doing was wrong, he knew, yet he felt powerless to stop it.

Perhaps he could have resisted her. Kept his distance. Done the right thing, if only he hadn't sensed such an emptiness in her. An emptiness that obviously his brother was not filling. An emptiness he knew only too well in his own heart. But that didn't make it right. A stab of conscience pierced his heart as he hungrily crushed her mouth beneath his and attempted to bury his guilt.

But it was futile.

Battling his conscience, Buck was a man torn. This woman in his arms—no matter how urgently she responded to him, no matter how desperately he wanted her, no matter how perfectly their mouths blended—still belonged to his brother. His *brother*, for pity's sake. A member of his family. His own flesh and blood. Mac.

The special brother who'd once saved his life. Emitting a tortured gasp, he tore his lips from hers and, angling their foreheads together, breathed heavily against the side of her face.

"We have to stop," he groaned, agonized.

"Yes," she whispered unconvincingly, her mouth brushing his.

She nipped at his lips with hers, nuzzling, tasting him, chinking away at his diminishing armor of decency. "Yes."

Buck groaned. They had to get back to the house, he thought foggily. Oh, man. They had to get back to the house, but quick. She kissed his chin, and the spot at the base of his throat where his heart attempted to hammer its way to freedom. Their bodies were pressed together, her delicate curves fitting his harder lines so naturally it boggled his mind. Oh, have mercy, she was made for him, and he for her; it was obvious. But that didn't make what they were doing any less troubling. On tiptoe, she arched against him and kissed the underside of his jaw.

Plunging his hands into her hair, he tugged her mouth back up to his for one final, emotion-packed kiss. One last, heated kiss that he could remember her by in the years to come. A kiss so hot that it would keep his cold and lonely heart warm in his old age. Because if there was one thing he knew without a doubt, it was that he would never, ever, find anyone who affected him the way Holly did.

Holly.

His future sister-in-law.

Oh, good Lord in heaven, what was he doing?

Buck gripped her arms and, backing up a step, set her away from his body. There he stood, unspeakably tempted, valiantly clinging to the last shred of his waning control.

This never should have happened.

This could never happen again.

A determined muscle jumped in his jaw as they gazed in surprise and horror at each other. Consumed with shame, Buck turned her around and grasped her arms from behind. "Come on," he commanded darkly, and, opening the passenger door to his truck, propelled her inside. "We've got to get you back to the house." Slamming the door, he added under his breath, "Before I change my mind."

Chapter Six

Later that evening, Holly pressed her cheek against the cool glass of the French paned doors that led to her veranda and watched the scene below with a heavy heart. The impromptu barbecue that Big Daddy had thrown was an unmitigated success. Friends and neighbors had flocked to the sprawling, festively decorated rose gardens to share in the frivolities. Paper lanterns cast a romantic glow against the statuary and topiary, and the fountain was lit with a pale gold light.

Several sides of beef roasted on spits over large barbecue pits that were fashioned just for the occasion, and chicken and pork ribs sizzled from grills in surrounding areas. Long tables, laden with all manner of Texas picnic-style fare, were lined with a multitude of people busily loading their plates. The guests, laughing and chatting happily, moved to picnic tables covered with red checked cloths, and in the background, one of Big Daddy's favorite local country-and-western bands softly crooned love ballads.

As these rhyming words of unrequited love filtered in three-part harmony up through Holly's open window, she closed her eyes and felt as if her heart would break.

Buck was down there, still apparently enjoying the party.

But she'd left.

She'd had to. She couldn't take any more of the furtive, questioning glances they'd exchanged across the crowded garden. After spending an obligatory hour feigning composure and trying to avoid insipid chitchat with people she did not know about an engagement that did not exist, she'd pleaded a headache and fled.

Not that it had mattered one way or another to Buck. He hadn't spoken to her on the way home from their—she cringed—tryst. Nor had he given her the time of day that evening, choosing instead to concentrate on a buxom blonde named Rhonda. And who could blame him? She was beautiful. A Christie Brinkley look-alike, with a dazzling personality to boot. Holly felt positively duller than day-old dishwater next to the lovely, effervescent Rhonda.

Opening her eyes, Holly looked down into the shadowed party until she found the table she was looking for. She focused on the laughing, bubbly Rhonda for a moment, and then the young woman's hand as it lay resting lightly on Buck's bicep. Her gaze strayed to Buck, and her heart slammed against her ribs at the memory of their heated kiss. Lightly, she ran her fingertips over her lower lip and sighed. It was obvious from the way he ignored her and fawned over Rhonda that he wished their kiss had never happened. Probably it had been an attempt at sympathy gone haywire. Her throat closed at the thought.

He didn't want her. He wanted Rhonda. And should that surprise her? After all, she was engaged to his brother. His *brother,* for heaven's sake. What must he think of her? The abandon with which she responded to him, clung to him, encouraged him. He must think she was every kind of fool, crying on his shoulder and practically begging to be kissed. What kind of woman would do that to her fiancé? With the man's brother, no less?

Thank heavens she hadn't had the opportunity to tell him the truth about her relationship with Mac. Telling him that she was a liar as well as a hussy would probably only have compounded problems.

"Ohh," she moaned in misery, and pressed her flaming cheeks to the glass to cool them. She could hardly wait for Mac to return. Because the moment he did, she thought fiercely, she was going to announce the truth to the world whether he liked it or not, and apologize to everyone for the pain she'd caused.

Sighing, Holly came to the bittersweet realization that it had all worked out according to plan, after all. No act would be required to portray a grieving, brokenhearted daughter to her meddling parents now. Yes, she would pack her bags, fly back to Oklahoma and bury herself in her work at Miracle House.

And, most likely, spend the rest of her life missing Buck.

"And that's how I got Bootsie!" Rhonda gushed, lifting her heavy golden mane off her neck and filtering the long strands through her fingertips. Swinging her head from side to side, she seemed to enjoy giving her hair a regular opportunity to take flight, much to the chagrin of those eating around her. Oblivious to this annoying habit, she bubbled on. "He's a ferret, too. I call him Bootsie because of the white boots on his feet. Isn't that cute?"

"Mmm."

"He's such a cuddly thing. I let him sleep with me and Precious, my other ferret. They eat off my plate and everything." Yet again flipping back her bleached and wavy mane, Rhonda revealed her pearly smile and batted her eyes coquettishly at Buck. "They are so adorable together. At Christmastime, I take them to the photographer and have their picture taken with Santa, and buy them tons of presents. They even have their own little tree. Isn't that cute?"

"Cute," Buck muttered, and tried to smile through the marching band that paraded through his temples. But it was tough. Rhonda had more cute rodent stories than Carter's had pills. All she had talked about all evening was her mangy menagerie of mutts.

"Oh, if you think that's cute, you should see their matching sweaters!" Rhonda burbled. "I know a lot of people don't think ferrets make very good pets, but once you get to know their little personalities, you just can't resist them."

"Really."

"Oh, sure. They're just like you and me. In fact, once, before I got Bootsie, I think Precious was depressed. She just moped around all day long and didn't touch her food. I was really worried, so I called a pet therapist…"

"Therapist?"

"Of course. Animals are people, too," she said, and nodded solemnly. "And he told me that he thought Precious was lonely." Tossing her head, she sent a shock wave of gold cascading in all directions around the table and a couple beside Rhonda lifted their plates out of the line of fire. Dipping her chin, Rhonda pouted prettily at Buck. "In fact, just the other day I went somewhere without her, just for a few minutes, mind you—"

Pasting a tolerant smile on his face, Buck tuned

Rhonda out as she continued her lengthy and enthusiastic diatribe on the mental health of her Precious, and allowed his thoughts to drift to Holly. Idly, he compared the two women.

Holly gave of her time and energy to hungry children. In fact, she was willing to postpone her own happiness for the sake of others in need. A deep sense of pride swelled in his gut. Holly was an amazing woman.

Rhonda spoiled rodents.

Glancing up at Holly's balcony, he searched for her to no avail and sighed. Why did fate deal him this hand? he wondered morosely, and allowed his gaze to settle on Rhonda's full, perfectly sculpted lips as she endlessly extolled the virtues of her darling pets. Holly was twice the woman that Rhonda was. Not that Rhonda was a bad person, he thought charitably, groping for some kind of silver lining in this hideous thundercloud that had become his life. She was pretty, charming and perkier than Mary Poppins on antidepressants, but she was no Holly Ferguson.

Sometimes life just seemed so unfair. Mac had no concept of what a lucky man he was. It was incomprehensible to Buck that his brother could just up and leave Holly to fend for herself the way he had. Especially without calling once for the entire two weeks he'd been gone. Buck knew that if Holly were his fiancée, he'd never let her out of his sight. Ever. One kiss was all it had taken for Buck to know that if she were engaged to him, he would be up there with her right now, further exploring the electricity that popped and crackled between them.

But Holly wasn't his. Never would be. And as far as he could tell, she hated him now. That didn't surprise him. After all, what on earth must she think of a man who would take advantage of his *brother's* intended bride that way? Unfair advantage no less, in her moment of weakness.

Oh, he was lower than low.

Balling his fists, he vowed that it was finally time to stop feeling sorry for himself. It was time to get on with his life. He needed to get Holly out of his system, once and for all. He needed to find something else upon which to focus his pent-up energy. Something like…Rhonda. His eyes swept to her still-moving mouth.

"…to enter Precious in a beauty contest. So I took her picture with a little tiara and a ribbon that said Miss Precious going across here—" Rhonda stopped and gestured across her generous cleavage "—and I sent it in." She clapped her hands with delight and ran her fingers through the golden cloud, fluffing, combing, teasing and finally sending it flying over her shoulder with a practiced swish that had Buck arching back to avoid being hit. "But I won't find out if she's a finalist for a while. I can't wait!"

Wincing, Buck shook his head to clear it of the mind-blowing image and decided to plunge in before he could change his mind. "How would you like to go out with me tomorrow night?" he suddenly heard himself asking. Mentally he crossed his fingers, hoping she would be busy. Most people had Saturday night all sewn up months in advance. Especially someone as pretty as Rhonda.

"Me?" Rhonda's long hair billowed out behind her as she snapped a thrilled look at Buck. "I'd *love* to," she accepted immediately, and flashed him a thousand-watt smile.

"I know it's kind of last minute and all…"

"No, really, it's fine. I don't have any plans."

"Great," Buck said, trying to inject a note of optimism

into his voice. "I thought maybe we could catch a show or something."

"Super! I hear there is a great one playing down at the drive-in outside Dallas."

"The drive-in?" Spending the evening confined in the cab of his pickup listening to the continuing escapades of Bootsie and Precious wasn't exactly his cup of tea, but he figured he had to start somewhere.

"Oh, sure. You'll love it!" Tossing her head, she lobbed a golden tendril across his nose. "They're playing *The Amazing Wilderness Trek*. It's about these adorable little doggies who get lost in the wilderness and have to find their way home through incredible odds. I just know you'll love it," she squealed, bouncing in her seat, swishing her hair back over her shoulder, "the animal lover that you are."

"Mmm." Buck was an animal lover all right. He loved the kind he could ride or brand, and that was about the extent of it. But what the hell. He'd keep an open mind. After all, what did he have to lose? "I'll pick you up at seven-thirty?"

"We'll be ready."

Holly tucked her legs up under her as she made herself comfortable in the overstuffed chair and gratefully accepted the after-dinner cup of coffee Miss Clarise offered her. Saturday evenings in the Brubaker household were a laid-back affair. Most of the boys had dates, or other planned activities, and Miss Clarise and Big Daddy would gather with whoever didn't in the family room for coffee, dessert and after-dinner conversation. Holly knew dress was casual, hence the denim shorts and baggy sweatshirt she wore pushed up to her elbows. Her hair was swept back into a loose ponytail, and her face was scrubbed clean of makeup.

Why bother primping? she had wondered, feeling lethargic and despondent. Buck had avoided her like the plague all day long, and Mac was still missing in action. For heaven's sake, getting all gussied up for an evening spent having a cup of coffee, then retiring alone to her room, seemed pointless. Besides, she didn't have the energy for anything more taxing than laying on her bed and crying.

Big Daddy and Miss Clarise cuddled in a love seat across the spacious and comfortable family room, sipping their coffee and speaking in the soft, low tones that spoke of a lifetime of love. Since she was the only other person in the room, Holly almost felt like an intruder as she listened to their playful flirtations. With a heavy heart, she tried to picture herself at their age, but saw only a bleak, desolate hole where her future should have been. Her future with Buck.

The sound of footsteps in the hallway, just outside the columned arch that lead to the family room, brought Holly from her maudlin reverie. Her heart screeched to a stop as her eyes landed on the new arrival. Buck. He was standing, bathed in lamplight, just inside the doorway, and to Holly he'd never looked more handsome.

Their eyes collided for a tension-charged moment, and then, as if unable to sustain the contact, Buck glanced over at his curious parents.

"What are your plans tonight, boy?" Big Daddy asked, and set his cup down on the coffee table next to the love seat. Springing to his feet, he appraised his strapping son from across the room. "You're all duded up."

"I have a date tonight." Buck's gaze didn't falter from his father.

"Well, now," Big Daddy crowed jubilantly. "That's wonderful." A satisfied grin split his rubbery face. "With who?"

"Rhonda."

"Good! She seems like a nice little gal."

Holly bristled. Sure, she thought churlishly, if you liked the statuesque beauty-queen type.

"She's okay." Lifting a nonchalant shoulder, Buck continued to avoid Holly's eyes.

"What are your plans?"

"Thought we'd go to the drive-in and catch something."

The drive-in? Holly's antennae lifted and she felt her mouth pucker into a sour wad. The drive-in. Oh, he'd catch something all right. The drive-in was a veritable hotbed of hormonal iniquity, and everyone knew it. Unwanted visions of Buck and the beautiful Rapunzel entwined in a romantic clinch tortured her.

"Say," Big Daddy thundered as a flash of inspiration hit, "why don't y'all take Holly along so that she can have some fun?"

Clearly taken back, Buck's jaw dropped.

Holly blanched.

"How 'bout it, honey pie? Doesn't that sound like a kick in the head?" Big Daddy's hawklike eyes danced over to Holly.

Yes, Holly thought, feeling as if she had indeed been hit between the eyes. Reeling, she blinked rapidly and gathered her swirling thoughts. "Oh, no. Really," she chirped, and waved an airy hand. "You all don't have to worry about me. I'm just fine spending a quiet evening at home."

"Nonsense!" Big Daddy roared. "Why, I promised

your papa that I'd show y'all a good time this summer, and I aim to do just that."

"But I *am* having a good time," Holly protested weakly.

"Fiddlesticks! You call mopin' around here on a Saturday night with a couple of old fogies a good time? No way! Not when y'all can be out with the youngsters, enjoying yourself."

At a complete loss, Holly nervously twisted her engagement ring and tried not to hyperventilate. Oh my gosh. She'd rather ride across Texas on a rusty bicycle with flat tires than spend an evening at the drive-in with Buck and his date, she thought frantically, her mind groping for a plausible excuse. Unfortunately, Big Daddy had caught her off guard, and with Buck staring at her that way, she couldn't put two cohesive words together. "Bah, ahh, but... Uh, I—"

"Now none of that. It's a done deal, you hear? Besides, Miss Clarise and I were hopin' to have the house to ourselves for a while, if—" his furry brows bounced in a suggestive manner and Miss Clarise giggled girlishly "—you catch my drift. Now, get on with you. Shooo!"

"Oh, no." Holly's eyes darted wildly from Big Daddy to Buck, where she pleaded with him for help. However, his stony expression offered no assistance. "Why... why...I *couldn't* go. I'm not ready. It would take too long for me to dress. I wouldn't want them to miss any of the movie." She smiled brightly, hoping that settled it. After all, it was the truth. She certainly couldn't go out in public looking like some kind of pathetic waif, devoid of makeup and a decent set of clothes.

"Don't be silly, darlin'," Miss Clarise said softly. "Why you look pretty as a picture. Doesn't she, Buck?"

Angling his head, Buck allowed his gaze to settle once

again on Holly. "Yes." The word was barely audible, a whispered caress that touched her from across the room.

"Well, what are you waiting for?" Leaping over to Holly's chair, Big Daddy extended his hand and, with a strength that surprised her, had her on her feet and standing next to Buck in record time. "You kids have a good time now, and don't come back too early, if you get my meaning."

His teasing words had Miss Clarise softly chuckling again.

As if resigning himself to a night in hell, Buck sighed and angled his head toward the front door. "After you."

The armrest pressed against Holly's side in a most uncomfortable manner, but she was beyond caring. Wedged as she was between the terminally cheerful Rhonda and the door of Buck's pickup, she decided the pain of the latter was better than constantly having to dig long strands of bleached blond hair out of her eyes. And her nose. And mouth. Like a horsetail flicking flies, Rhonda's luxurious mane *swished* to and fro as she chatted first with Buck, then *swished* to Holly, then *swished-bounced-swished*, back to Buck. Unrolling his window, Buck leaned out and pretended to adjust the side mirror to avoid being slapped again.

Much to Rhonda's credit, she hadn't batted an eyelash over Holly's presence when they'd arrived at her door. Instead, she'd adopted a "more the merrier" attitude as she'd squeezed into the cozy spot on the pickup's bench seat between Holly and Buck. Which, Holly mused, must explain the presence of Precious, the droopy ferret, poking her curious nose from the confines of Rhonda's purse.

"I thought a night out on the town might cheer her up," Rhonda had explained on the way to the drive-in as she cooed and patted the sad-eyed rodent. Tossing her cloud of wonderful, silky blond hair over her shoulder, she shrugged. *Swish. Swish.* "She's been kind of down lately."

I can identify, Holly thought, pulling a strand of Rhonda's blond mane out of her mouth and warily eyeing the fur ball that was now flopped dramatically across Rhonda's lap. Rhonda, per usual, kept up a nonstop line of chatter as they sped toward the drive-in, thankfully sparing Holly from having to engage her aching brain. Besides, Buck seemed only too happy to egg her on with monosyllabic words and interested grunts of encouragement.

Feeling positively dowdy, Holly allowed her gaze to wander over Rhonda's chic apparel and perfectly made-up face. Her slim-fitting white slacks and sleeveless sun top only served to enhance her graceful figure, and her long, lithe arms were tanned to a golden perfection. Costume jewelry jangled pleasantly at her slender wrists, and she smelled faintly of expensive perfume. Looking as though she'd just stepped from the pages of a fashion magazine, Rhonda exuded confidence and poise.

Holly, on the other hand, squirmed restlessly within the billowy recesses of her oversize sweatshirt, and wished she'd at least had time to run a comb through her hair and dab on some makeup.

When they'd at last reached the drive-in, paid the entry fee and parked, they sat, three—four counting Precious—cozy little peas in the pod from hell. The tension was thick enough to need a jackhammer, to everyone it seemed but Rhonda. Lolling her head listlessly against the cool glass of the window, Holly looked at the family in the car parked next to them and absently wondered if they would mind if she joined them.

"I'm going to go get us some popcorn," Buck finally announced when Rhonda paused for air. Unbuckling his seat belt, he opened the door and was out in a flash. "Want anything else?" he barked over his shoulder, already moving away from the truck.

"No thanks," Holly mumbled.

"Oh, honey," Rhonda said, "hurry. You won't want to miss a minute of the feature."

"I'll hurry," he promised, and disappeared into the shadows.

With a swish of her hair, Rhonda turned in her seat and beamed at Holly. "I'm so glad you could join us tonight."

Holly brushed a golden strand from her eyes and smiled weakly at Rhonda. "I feel like I'm intruding."

"Oh, don't be a goose." Rhonda's tinkly laughter filled the cab. "I've been wanting to get to know you a little better."

"Why is that?" Holly asked, perplexed.

"Well, if everything works out between me and Buck, we could be sisters-in-law someday."

"Sisters-in-law?" Holly choked.

"Why sure. You are engaged to Mac, aren't you?"

"Uh, well…"

"Well—" Rhonda clapped, pep-rally fashion "—there you go."

"Are you saying that, uh, you want to, uh, marry Buck?" Holly asked, feeling suddenly nauseated.

"Who wouldn't?" Buck's date pretended to swoon. "Isn't he just the dreamiest? And he'd make such a good father to Precious here—" she stroked the ferret's drowsy head "—and, of course, Bootsie."

"Bootsie?"

"My other ferret. He has the cutest little white feet,

with brown legs and a little pink freckle on his nose. Isn't that cute?''

"Cute." Too stunned to comment further, Holly tried to reconcile the numbing picture in her mind's eye of Buck as he—a look of paternal bliss on his face—joggled a fur wad named Bootsie on his knee. It was too much to contemplate at this juncture.

"Oh, but not as cute as Buck. I know you must feel the same way about Mac. Aren't we lucky? They are so handsome, don't you think? So...manly." Her lilting laughter trilled the scales. "I just love his hair. Hair is a really big deal to me..."

Until it begins to fall out, Holly thought in irritation. What then?

As Rhonda needlessly extolled Buck's many virtues to her, Holly began to have an out-of-body experience. Feeling as if she were floating, she looked down at this ridiculous scene and tried to bite back a wave of hysterical laughter. What was she doing here, caught in this absurd triangle? And why on earth, she wondered, knitting her brow in consternation, had she promised to keep Mac's secret? Suddenly none of this nutty charade made any sense.

The age-old phrase "When at first we practice to deceive" flitted through her head. Oh, she'd woven a tangled web, all right. And she needed to stop. Now, she thought with determination. She needed to pack her bags and go home to Oklahoma. Obviously Buck was intent on getting on with his life, as was Mac. They didn't need her here, complicating matters. She was nothing more than a third wheel on life's bicycle. Well, enough was enough.

As Rhonda continued to natter endlessly on about Buck's attributes, Holly tried to hate Rhonda, but couldn't. None of this was her fault. She was entitled to date Buck. She was single, beautiful and full of...of...pep. They should be together. And she...well, she should face the inevitable now.

Mac was clearly in no big hurry to come back, and she couldn't live in limbo like this anymore. Come Monday morning, she was packing her bags and heading back to her old life. A life of safety. A life of fulfillment.

A life of loneliness.

And if this decision didn't give her any peace, at least it gave her some direction.

At long last, the wretched *Amazing Wilderness Trek* ended, and with the exception of Precious returning from the dead and freaking out over the movie's many and varied sound effects, no harm was done. Buck glanced ruefully down at the sticky puddle of soda and popcorn that now graced his once pristine floorboards and sighed as he sped toward Rhonda's house to drop her off. It was amazing how much the little ferret had hated the snapping, snarling growls of the Alaskan grizzly. Arching toward the steering wheel, he rotated his shoulders and tried to shake off the feeling that a rodent was still clutching him by the throat.

Thank heavens Holly traveled solo.

Holly.

His eyes darted over to her, but she was leaning against the passenger door sleeping. Or at least pretending to. Probably simply trying to avoid Rhonda's nonstop patter. Buck raked a hand over his face as he nodded at something or another Rhonda was saying. Man, oh, man. For a woman who claimed she couldn't wait to see the damn movie, she hadn't shut up for more than a minute since he'd picked her up.

The whole evening, he'd ached to touch Holly. Several times he'd put his arm over Rhonda's shoulders, only in a vain attempt to reach Holly. To feel the warmth that radiated from her. To feel the silky softness of her hair. To connect with her, somehow.

But she hadn't reacted. Instead, she'd sat like a bump on a log. With the exception, he thought with a small smile, of the times Precious decided to gallop around the cab, building a crazy kind of centrifugal force that even Rhonda seemed at a loss to control.

Yeah, that had had Holly looking to him for help. Eyes wide, and hands frantically clutching his shirt, she had screamed, "Get it, Buck! Quick! Quick! Do something!"

Buck smiled. There had been at least one bright spot to the evening.

"Right here," Rhonda directed, pointing to her street as they approached. "I think we lost Holly," she whispered.

"Mmm," Buck agreed, darting a glance at Holly. She looked so angelic, nestled into the corner of the cab that way, her heavy lashes resting lightly on her cheeks, her smooth skin alabaster in the streetlight. She was a real beauty. Not overly polished, like Rhonda, but fresh-faced and bright-eyed and full of love and concern for her fellow man. Buck's heart swelled at the sight.

"It was so nice to have a chance to get to know her a little tonight," Rhonda continued in her confidential whisper. "I bet she's really anxious for Mac to come home."

"Mmm."

"She can probably hardly wait to see him. I know it must be hard on her, being away from her true love for so long."

"Mmm." Buck squirmed uncomfortably.

"So how are the wedding plans coming? Are they going on a romantic honeymoon somewhere? I always thought a lush, tropical island would be my first choice. But I don't really think it matters where you are, as long as you are snuggled up *together!*" She sighed. "For the whoooole night to finally be able to do—"

"Here we are." Rhonda's innocent prattle had Buck ready to throttle someone. Applying a less than subtle pressure to the brake, Buck ground to a stop at the curb and gestured to her house.

"Home sweet home."

"Wow. That was quick!" Rhonda praised.

With a no-nonsense shove, Buck pushed open his door and helped Rhonda to the street. Grabbing the nervous Precious, he deposited the mutt into her mistress's arms and propelled them rapidly down the walk and up the steps of her front porch.

Holly hated herself for peeking, but she couldn't seem to resist the temptation. Morbid fascination, most likely. Her heart began to pound most uncomfortably beneath her breast as Buck escorted Rhonda up the porch stairs to her house and retreated into the shadowy light that the solitary bulb provided.

Through the crack in the truck's window, Holly could hear Buck's low murmured words, and a giddy giggle from Rhonda accompanied by some more flirtatious hair swishing. Sitting up straight and lowering the window a little more, Holly strained to make out the scene that both tortured and fascinated her.

As Buck's lips brushed Rhonda's mouth in a most perfunctory kiss, Holly felt as if she'd been stabbed in the heart. Unable to rip her eyes from the scene that played out before her, she wriggled in her seat and seethed, and considered rushing up the steps and scratching Rhonda bald.

But what good would that do? Buck had every right to date whomever he wanted. To kiss whomever he wanted. With the one exception of her. She had no right to feel so possessive over his kisses. Buck deserved far better than her. He deserved far better than Rhonda, as far as she was concerned, but she was in no position to make suggestions, she thought morosely. Well, soon enough she would be back home and all this would be behind her. A big, horrible memory that someday she would be able to laugh at. Hopefully.

The sound of boots rumbling down the porch's steps signaled Buck's eminent return. Slinking down into her corner of the truck, Holly quickly closed her eyes and tried to slow her breathing to the appearance of sleep. As he pulled open his door, she could sense Buck regarding her for a moment, probably resentfully thinking that if it wasn't for her he could be with Rhonda right now, becoming better acquainted with those full, perfectly sculpted—and, she thought sourly, constantly flapping—lips.

The bright Texas moon filtered softly into the cab with Buck as he slid into the cab, and paused for a moment to regard Holly. It was amazing how different two women could be. He'd made an honest effort back there with Rhonda. But there were simply no sparks. No passion. No fire.

Not like a kiss with Holly.

Aw, well, he thought, and, with a shake of his head, ran a hand over his jaw. He could have figured that one out for himself. Nobody did it for him like Holly Ferguson. Sighing, he started the engine and pulled away from the curb without a backward glance at Rhonda, and they drove home in complete silence.

Chapter Seven

The following morning found the entire Brubaker clan—with the noticeable exception of Mac and Buck—relaxing outdoors in the rose garden at Sunday brunch. A large brick patio, surrounded by box hedges, prizewinning roses, various and sundry water fountains and Greek statuary made up the outdoor dining area. Numerous side tables, covered in white linen, held silver serving dishes loaded with some of the most spectacular creations Holly had ever seen or smelled.

She'd have been salivating if she hadn't been so sick at heart. One table's sole purpose—she noted limply—was to hold the ice sculpture. Sunlight filtered into this private oasis, mingling with the mellow strains of baroque chamber music provided by the outdoor stereo system.

Sunday brunch, Miss Clarise insisted, was the one meal where she could count on gathering all her chicks together and enjoying their company. This week, she was tickled to host Bru and Penelope, as well as Holly. Since

Patsy was still in Europe studying dance, she relished the feminine company.

The whole brood was still decked out in their Sunday best after the morning's church service as they took their seats at the long, beautifully appointed table. The only cloud to mar this otherwise perfect occasion for Miss Clarise was the continuing and mysterious absence of Mac, and now—even more disconcerting—the sudden disappearance of Buck immediately after church.

"Holly, darlin'," Miss Clarise's soft voice murmured from directly across the table nearly midway through the meal, "do you have any idea where Buck might have disappeared to after church this mornin'?"

"Me?" Holly asked, flushing. She glanced awkwardly around. She hadn't spoken to Buck since he'd dropped her at the front door last night after their debacle of a date at the drive-in with Rhonda and Precious. Once they'd arrived home, she'd no sooner stepped out of the truck and turned to make amends for ruining his evening when, without so much as a good-night grunt, he'd sped off to the parking area at the other side of the house. There he'd screeched to a stop, leapt out of his truck, slammed the door and bounded off toward the stable.

Holly had watched from the front porch, near the mansion's front door, as he'd retreated to the shadowed interior of the stable, hoping to have a word with him. She had waited for a quarter of an hour, to no avail, for his return. Finally, slumping in defeat, she'd pushed off the railing and shuffled inside to bed. It was clear that he'd been eager to get rid of her, she thought bleakly, considering how she'd horned in on his opportunity to spend some private time with the delectable and endlessly perky Rhonda.

Well, perky Rhonda and her peppy pets could just have

him. The catty thought had done little to cheer her, and
as she'd slogged up the stairs to her room, painful tears
had pricked the backs of her eyes. Throat aching, she'd
sniffed noisily at the injustice of it all. What a fool she'd
been this whole summer. If she hadn't lied to everyone
about being engaged to Mac, she wouldn't be looking for
an escape route from this three-ring circus, but perhaps,
instead, exploring a real relationship with the third Brubaker son. The son she should have been seeing all along.

Biting back an uncharacteristic flood of tears, Holly
left her ruminations and returned to the present. Squaring
her shoulders, she stoically answered Miss Clarise. "Uh,
no, ma'am. He didn't mention anything to me about his
plans this morning."

"Oh, dear." Miss Clarise glanced pensively at her
watch, then at Holly. "Oh my." A fretful look crossed
her lovely face as she again checked her watch, then
leaned forward to whisper in Big Daddy's ear.

"What the devil?" Big Daddy bellowed over a mouthful of toast, and craned his neck, searching in disbelief
for his other absent son. "You mean he's not here, either? Well, what in tarnation are we gonna tell—"

"Big Daddy," Miss Clarise whispered quellingly.

Sighing, he rolled his eyes in disgust and lamented
under his crumb-sputtering breath how "heads were
gonna roll." Tossing his toast onto his plate, he growled,
"For pity's sake. He would be late, today of all days."
Harrumphing, he glanced surreptitiously at Holly, then
barked at his wife, "Well, we gotta find him." Stuffing
his hand into his vest he withdrew his gold pocket watch,
flipped it open and narrowed his brow and muttered,
"What the heck is the matter with that boy? For that
matter, what the devil's the matter with Mac?" Glancing

sheepishly at Penelope and Holly he said, "Pardon my French, ladies."

Penelope shifted to a more comfortable position in her chair and smiled at her father-in-law. "Big Daddy, perhaps Buck had some work to attend to? I think I saw him headed out the South Section road when Bru and I pulled up," she volunteered.

"Workin'? On the day of rest? Oh, for the love of—" Big Daddy roared, and snapped shut his pocket watch. To Miss Clarise he muttered, "Lookie, honey pie, we're runnin' outta time here, and we need to get organized. Somebody's gotta go get that boy and bring him back here now."

"I will," Bru offered, his hand resting lightly on his pregnant wife's belly. The baby had been especially active that morning, and Penelope was threatening to start charging members of the family for their curious and delighted probings of her burgeoning midsection.

"No. You stay here with your woman," Big Daddy commanded. "Can't go runnin' all over tarnation with her in that condition."

Bru and Penelope exchanged amused glances.

"Perhaps Holly could help," Miss Clarise suggested, glancing meaningfully at Big Daddy. Turning, she cast an innocent glance at Holly. "You know where the South Section is, don't you, darlin'? Maybe you could go summon Buck back to the house for some, uh, er, brunch." Her creamy complexion went pink.

"That's the perfect solution," Big Daddy crowed, his beady eyes lighting at the suggestion. "Holly, you go fetch that boy, and bring him back here."

"Bu-bu—" Holly stammered, horrified at the idea.

"Yes," Miss Clarise breathed, shooting Big Daddy a

grateful look. "That would solve a multitude of problems, wouldn't it?"

"Yep." Big Daddy grunted. "Perfect solution."

"Oh. I... You want, uh, *me* to, uh, go out to the South Section and tell Buck to come back to the house?" Again? She thought, her heart sinking. Please say no, she silently pleaded. Please send someone else. Anyone else. Holly felt her mouth go dry and her heart rebound from her shoes and forge its way into her throat. She remembered only too clearly what running out to the South Section to fetch Buck had gotten her into last time.

"Yes, dear, that's precisely right," Miss Clarise said, and beamed. "In fact, the sooner you bring him back, the sooner we can begin...our...day!"

Holly glanced around the table, only to find all eyes trained expectantly on her.

Something was up.

Yep, something was rotten in River City, or Denver, or Denmark, or wherever it was that things went rotten. For some reason, they wanted Buck back here on the double. And, for some other reason, they wanted to get rid of her.

Her heart skipped a terrified beat. Did they know? Did they know about her pretend engagement to Mac? Did they know about her feelings for Buck? Feeling panicky, she darted fearful glances between Big Daddy and Miss Clarise and then down at her hands as she rotated her phony engagement ring. Were they plotting some kind of retaliation for the wool she'd pulled over all their eyes?

Squeezing her eyes tightly shut, she knew that she deserved whatever they were obviously planning. It served her right. She had no problem with taking her lumps and admitting that she'd been wrong. Very, very wrong.

She just hadn't wanted it to end this way.

She wanted to be the one to confess the ridiculous truth. To throw herself at their mercy and grovel for forgiveness. But she didn't want to do it until much later in the day when she could take them aside in private and bare her soul, telling them the whole sorry story from beginning to end.

Inhaling deeply, she opened her eyes and cast her gaze to the senior Brubakers. They were smiling. Not angry, just smiling expectantly, waiting for her to run off and fetch Buck.

Taking a deep breath, she returned their smile and tried to still her overactive imagination. Okay. Good. They were still smiling. Perhaps there was a chance that they didn't know. Perhaps this wasn't about her at all. Perhaps they simply had some family business to discuss and needed Buck to be present. Well, in any event, she could do this simple task for them. Especially considering how gracious they'd been to her all summer. Flames of guilt scorched her already charred conscience.

Going to fetch Buck was the least she could do. In fact, it would probably be one of the last things she would be able to do for them, being that tomorrow—provided she lived that long—she was going to be packing her bags and heading back to Oklahoma.

Yes, tonight she would draw Miss Clarise and Big Daddy aside and tell them the awful truth. Beg them not to blame Mac or to go running after him. They would have to come to terms with the fact that it was Mac's life now. He was a grown man, with a wife out there somewhere that he was trying to protect.

She would try to help them understand that.

She would try to help them understand why she had told such a passel of lies to everyone. Wincing, her heart sank at the thought of their crumpled faces. What had started out as a lark, as a simple practical joke, had turned into a hole so deep, so complex and so pathetically wrong, she feared she'd never be able to dig her way out.

After she'd come clean with the older couple, when she had a chance she would pull Buck aside and tell him the truth, as well. He would hate her, of course, for lying to him all this time, but, she thought morosely, that was nothing new. Maybe someday, in time, he could forgive her. They could be...friends. Perhaps she could add Buck and Rhonda to her Christmas card list, and keep up with them, and their...ferrets.

The very thought made her blood run cold.

She should be Buck's wife. Not Rhonda.

"Yes," she suddenly blurted out. "I'll go fetch him." Miserable or not, at least it was a chance to spend a few last minutes in his company. Alone.

"Wonderful, darlin'! That's so sweet." Miss Clarise once again glanced in concern at her watch. "If you don't mind leaving right after you've finished up, perhaps you can have him back just in time to—"

"Have a little brunch," Big Daddy supplied.

"Yes. Brunch." Miss Clarise smiled.

Lifting her shoulders in resignation, Holly tossed her napkin on the table and stood on wobbly legs. "Well," she warbled, trying to sound relaxed and confident, "I'll...just go rustle him up."

"That's a good girl," Big Daddy exclaimed, then pulling a pen from his pocket, furiously scribbled a few words. "Here, honey, give this to him."

As she made her way out of the rose garden, she could hear the escalating camaraderie, excited whispers and hushed exclamations of a close-knit family finally able to enjoy some time to themselves, unencumbered by outsiders.

Yes, she thought, filled with sadness. Something was going on. Something that obviously did not include her. A hollow feeling settled in the pit of her stomach, suddenly making her feel more alone than she ever had before in her life.

Of course, Buck's attitude didn't help matters much at all.

"What is it?" He sighed, pulling to a stop at the side of the road in the South Section, next to where she'd been shuffling toward him through the dust. Rolling down his window the rest of the way, he watched her approach.

Holly bristled at the impatient note in his voice. This had not been her idea, running all over heck and gone in this sweltering heat, looking for him. Just as it had not been her idea to horn in on his little love nest with Rhonda last night. "Your father sent you a note," she snapped, sounding a little more churlish than she'd intended. Gracious, he was a sight for sore eyes.

Buck glanced at her hand and snorted. "Another note?"

Unable to control it, Holly felt a smile tug at her mouth. "Yes. Another one."

"Well, I haven't got time for another damn barbecue," he groused, as if it were all her fault.

Engine idling, Buck reached out the driver's side window of his pickup truck, took the envelope from Holly's hand, ripped it open and quickly scanned its contents. Sighing heavily, he reached across the cab of the truck and shoved open the passenger door. "Get in."

"No thank you," she primly declined. "I'm perfectly capable of walking home on my own. I found my way out here, didn't I?" She would be far better off out here with the rattlesnakes than in the cab of that truck with a man she simply had no power left to resist. It wasn't fair to him. Or to her. Or to Rhonda and her ferrets, for that matter. Soon enough, she would confess the ugly truth about her pathetic love for him, and apologize for any inconvenience or embarrassment she may have caused. It was the perfect solution for everyone.

With an fluttery hand, she forced a carefree smile and waved him away. "You just go on."

Looping his arms over the steering wheel, Buck rested his head on the backs of his wrists. "Just spare me this grief and get in, will you?"

"But why do I have to go back now? I don't feel like eating."

"Who knows? The note just says for me to bring you back to the house with me, and that's what I intend to do."

"Buck, I don't think they mean for you to bring me. I think they are trying to get *rid* of me. That's why they sent me out here, to find you. It's *you* they want. It's you they were asking for."

Exasperated, Buck lolled his head and squinted at her. "Holly, by now you should know that my parents always mean what they say. Especially my father." He crumpled the paper tightly in his fist. "The note says to bring you back, so just get in."

"No." She was not going to spend another minute in his company unchaperoned. She couldn't trust herself not to do something that she would remember with extreme embarrassment for the rest of her life.

"Holly," he muttered, and gunned his engine loudly so that she jumped. Lifting his head, he scowled in an ominous fashion and growled.

Something in his voice carried a warning that she

dared not ignore. "Fine," she barked, and flounced—her sun skirt whirling in the dust—over to the passenger door, yanked it open and flopped into the seat next to Buck. "Happy now?" she asked sarcastically and slammed the door.

"Mmm." Jaw jumping, he shifted his truck into gear and began to bounce down the bumpy road that lead from the South Section to the main house.

To Holly it seemed that he was going out of his way to hit every pothole this section had to offer. "Ouch. For heaven's sake, Buck, you're giving me whiplash."

"Tighten your belt," he gritted out.

"What's the bee in your bonnet?" Holly snapped.

"I might ask you the same question."

"What's that supposed to mean?"

His jaw twitched as he groped for an accusation. "Well, for starters, you weren't exactly friendly to Rhonda last night."

"What?" Holly gasped, offended. "I was perfectly friendly to that rat-carrying amazon."

"Oh, yeah?" Buck taunted, fighting a grin at her feisty words. "Well, you sure didn't act like it, ignoring her through most of the movie, sulking in your corner. At least she had the decency to try to draw you out."

"Is that what you call her nonstop blather? Drawing me out?" Holly bristled as she twisted in her seat and thrust her chin out at Buck.

"She was making an effort."

"And I wasn't?" Holly sidled up against the door and fumed. "What about you? If you found her so fascinating, why did you spend more time at the popcorn counter than paying attention to her?"

His eyes glittered dangerously. "What are you trying to say?"

"Just that you didn't seem any more enthusiastic about your date with Rhonda than I was." Lifting her shoulders, Holly eyed his grim profile. Why was she goading him this way? It was obvious that he preferred the beautiful Rhonda over her. But, alas, once the words started tumbling, she was helpless to hold them back. "I mean, after all, the good-night kiss you gave her at the door was pretty…"

"Yes?" The stable finally came roaring into view, and seeming intent on making up for lost time, Buck put the pedal to the metal. "Go on," he ground out, narrowing his frustrated gaze on her. "What about the good-night kiss?"

"Well, it was…was—ouch! Slow down!" Reaching forward, she braced herself on the dash. "It was pretty pathetic, if you must know."

"Pathetic?" His jaw dropped as he groped for a snappy comeback that would not come. "How would you know that? I thought you were asleep!"

"Wrong-o, Buck-o! And—ouch—what I saw was pa-pa-thet-ic—ouch!" she chattered as they flew through the potholes, her head thudding most annoyingly against the door. "Buck, slow down! You're going to get us killed!"

Jamming on the brakes, Buck screeched to a stop in the parking area near the stable and threw open his door. Before Holly knew what hit her, he'd rounded the front of his rig, ripped open her door, hauled her out of the cab and pinned her against the truck's bed.

"Pathetic?" he growled against her lips.

"Yes," she snapped, squirming in his iron grasp.

"Well, then, Little Miss Know-it-all, how would you have had me kiss her?"

"With…with…the…" Holly gasped as he once again

crushed her between the warm metal of the truck's bed and the warm steel of his body. "With the...passion of someone who is in love," she flung at him.

"Like this?" he growled, yanking her roughly against his chest and giving her the kiss they'd both been dying for.

"Yes," she gasped, twining her arms around his neck and straining toward him. "Yes! Yes...like...that," she murmured as her mouth melded perfectly with his.

"I can't," he muttered against her lips when he could speak again.

"Why?"

"Because I'm not in love with her. I—" he claimed her mouth for another mind-bending moment, then continued brokenly "—could never kiss a woman this way if I didn't...love her."

Holly stilled in his arms. "Really?" Her voice was tentative. Thready with emotion.

Groaning, he buried his face in her neck, filling his hands with her hair and inhaling the essence that was uniquely Holly. "Yes. That's why we can't do this. You are *engaged!* To my *brother,* Holly! We can't do this! Don't you see?" Agonized, his words were broken.

"Yes," she whispered urgently. "I mean, no! No, it's not what you think. I have to tell you the truth. But not here. It's such a long story."

Framing her face in his hands he pulled her nose to his and looked deeply into her eyes. "Tell me," he gritted out through his tightly clenched jaw. "Tell me *now*. Can't you see how this is killing me?" Spreading his legs for balance, he leaned against the side of his truck and drew her into his embrace, hungrily ravishing her mouth like a man on death row devouring his last meal.

"I can't!" she breathed into his mouth, clutching his

shoulders for support. "Not yet. Not until I have a chance to talk to your folks about something important."

"What? What is so important?" Clutching her arms, he gave her a gentle shake. "What is this secret you've been keeping from me?"

"I'll tell you as soon as I can, I swear. Don't you know it's killing me, too?" Eyes flashing, she searched his face and made a promise. "I will tell you the honest truth from beginning to end, tonight. Until then, just know that..." Moaning, she let his mouth steal her words for a moment. "Know that...I love..." Feeling dizzy, carried away by some swirling vortex that left her dazed and confused, Holly tried to confess her feeling to Buck. "You have to know that...I...love...you."

"What?" Buck murmured, nonplussed, even as he drew Holly farther into his embrace.

Somewhere in the back of their passion-induced fog, the sounds of a car door slamming reached their fuzzy brains.

"Ahem."

A loud, masculine throat cleared, rumbling just behind them.

Starting, they sprang guiltily apart and, trying to appear calm, cool and collected, turned to greet the person who must have seen everything.

Holly was the first to recover her senses.

"Oh. Hi, Daddy," she croaked, and allowed her forehead to thud forward on Buck's strong chest.

Chapter Eight

"Well, howdy, you two lovebirds!" George Ferguson's voice boomed like an old ship's cannon, causing Holly to clutch Buck's arm to keep from slipping to the ground in mortification. "Don't look so guilty!" he chortled gleefully. "Why, I kissed your mama a time or two before we tied the knot!" His ribald laughter rang out as he tugged his beaming wife over to where the young couple stood in slack-jawed and buggy-eyed shock.

"D-Daddy! I-I...didn't expect you till *next* weekend," Holly stammered, nonplussed. She shot a helpless look at Buck who, groping for the door of his truck for support, looked equally stunned.

"We wanted to surprise ya, sweetheart," he thundered, moving between the guilty pair and enveloping his trembling daughter in a bear hug.

George was an imposing man, as wide as he was tall. A ten-gallon hat perched atop his eleven-gallon head, and the high heels on his expensive boots only added to his impressive stature. His doughy face was upholstered with

deep smile grooves and fringed with longish silver wisps
of unruly hair that poked out in a rakish manner from
beneath the giant brim of his hat. A gaudy silver buckle
bobbed just beneath his belly when he laughed, and, at
the moment, it was getting a hearty workout.

Taking a step back, Buck watched Holly's parents
greet her and feverishly tried to decide the best way to
explain that he'd just been caught kissing his brother's
fiancée. His racing mind skimmed the absurd possibili-
ties. Perhaps he could say he was congratulating her on
her engagement? Or maybe he could say that he was
assisting her with a lost contact lens? Teaching her
mouth-to-mouth resuscitation? Helping with a loose filling? His heart sank like a rusty anchor. He was a dead
duck.

"Speaking of kissin'," Holly's father chortled, lifting
her face out of his hearty bosom, "give your daddy some
sugar, honey love! Boy howdy, how I've missed my little
gal! Just couldn't wait another week to kiss these precious cheeks." Grabbing Holly's face between his meaty
hands, George puckered up his fleshy lips and planted
some noisy and enthusiastic kisses on her cheeks and
forehead.

"And," Trudy put in excitedly as she patted Buck's
arm, "we couldn't wait to get reacquainted with you,
Merle! Why, it's nearly twenty years since we've seen
you last. Why, if I hadn't seen you kissing Holly with
such—" she fanned her pink cheeks with her hand
"—such...fervor, well, I'd never have recognized you!"

"Merle?" Buck croaked, and stared at Holly's mother,
not quite comprehending at first, then the dreaded truth
hit home. Oh, good night, nurse. They thought he was
Mac. Brows arched, he shot Holly a loaded look. He
couldn't let Holly's parents think he was Mac. Things

were complicated enough at the moment without giving them the wrong impression.

"Oh, no, ma'am, I'm not really Merle… There's been a terrible mistake. I'm—"

"Oh, I know," Trudy interrupted with an airy hand. "Big Daddy told us how all you boys hated the names he gave you, and go by nicknames. Let's see now. You like everyone to call you Max, is that right?"

"No! Not Max. It's—"

"Hmm. Mark?"

"No, no! Actually—"

"Oh, dear. Matt?"

"No! It's Mac." Buck vehemently shook his head as Trudy looked benignly on. "But, actually, I'm not Max or Mark or Matt or even Merle! Really, ma'am, I'd like to make that clear from the beginning. In fact—"

"That's okay, sweetheart," Trudy said with a careless shrug and a throaty giggle. "There are so many of you Brubaker boys, your names and nicknames have always been a muddle in my head. But I hear what you are saying, darlin'. I never did fancy myself as a Gertrude, or even a Gerty, if you know what I mean? I'm Trudy through and through. I say pick the name you like and go with it!" Her low alto liltingly shot the scales to soprano and back, her glee seeming to grab her by the shoulders and bob her to and fro. Then, sobering slightly, she winked conspiratorially at Buck. "Bet you never knew that Holly was named after Buddy Holly, did you?"

Momentarily at a loss in his momentum to set the record straight, Buck paused and grinned in spite of himself. "No, I can't say that I did."

Holly cradled her head in her hands and moaned.

"Holly hates it when we tell this story," her mother burbled good-naturedly.

Trudy Ferguson was a delightful mixture of girlish enthusiasm and Southern gentility and rollicking laughter. Somewhere in her early sixties, her short, curly hair was more salt than pepper, and on her it looked oddly youthful. Laugh lines forked at the corners of her eyes as she winked at Buck.

"Oh, yes," she continued, in spite of her daughter's obvious discomfort. "It was Big Daddy's idea that he, and George over here—" she gestured artlessly at her burly husband "—name all you children after country-and-western singers, so Holly it was." Her hearty mirth rang out. "It was either that or Elvis, and I just couldn't do that to my little girl. Luckily she was an only child, or I'm sure we'd have an Elvis Ferguson runnin' around somewhere." Again, her laughter, like Old Faithful, cascaded forth from the depths of her being. "So I understand more than anyone why you are sensitive about your name. How about if I just call you...son?" she suggested, looping her arm through his.

"Son it is!" George bellowed, and heartily clapped Buck on the back as he released Holly and enthusiastically embraced his future son-in-law against his well-padded torso. "Welcome to the family, boy!"

"Thank you, sir" came Buck's muffled reply, not sure exactly where he fit into this wacky family at this point. However, he knew that one way or another he would end up a relative of this man and aimed to set the record straight from the beginning. "But I feel I must tell you the truth. My name is not Ma—"

"Oh, sure, I know, all you kids go by nicknames. That's fine."

"But...bu—"

Unfortunately, before Buck could correct this mistaken identity problem, Big Daddy and Miss Clarise came rushing out of the house and bounding down the path that cut through the rolling lawn to greet their long-lost friends, yoo-hooing and hallooing so loudly they effectively drowned out their sputtering son.

And, have mercy, what a reunion. The tears. The shouting. The hugging and screaming with joy.

And that was just Big Daddy.

"There you are! Such a sight for sore eyes! You're late, George, you old goat," Big Daddy thundered, beaming like a miniature lighthouse on a foggy beach as he tackled his giant friend in an effusive hug. "Why, you nearly ruined the s-u-r-p-r-i-s-e!" He cast a furtive glance at the still-reeling Holly, then, grabbing Trudy, stood on tiptoe and gave the chortling woman a noisy lip smack on her flaming cheek. The four old cronies hugged and kissed and crowed the usual "it's been far too long" pleasantries.

"We're just sorry that Mac won't be attending the festivities," Big Daddy lamented to George, taking it for granted that Holly had filled her father in on Mac's absence. "But that's okay. This kind of social occasion never was his cup o' tea."

"Nonsense," George bellowed, and darted a quick glance back at his daughter who was busily clutching the love of her life and gazing up at him with eyes of adoration. "No need to worry about him. Mac's a big boy. He can take care of himself."

Big Daddy beamed. "Glad you see it that way, too, George old man!"

"In a way, I know just how the poor kid feels." George snorted. "When Trudy first hit me with this co-ed shower idea, it didn't set too well with me, either.

That's woman's stuff, I say. But—'' his face softened as he looked over at his wife ''—she was very persuasive. Holly is our only child and all.''

"Yep." Big Daddy's eyes grew moist. "And we're so happy to be sharin' her with you. The whole family just loves her to pieces."

"We're a lucky pair of sons o' guns." George sniffed and, blinking rapidly, clapped Big Daddy soundly on his back, nearly bowling the diminutive man over with his unrestrained emotion.

Momentarily forgotten in the reunion mayhem, Holly and Buck were left to themselves for a brief, private confab.

"What are we going to do?" Holly whispered urgently, looking plaintively at Buck as she grasped the front of his shirt and pulled his ear to her mouth. "My parents think you're Mac!"

"I know, I know! I tried to tell them I'm not, but they kept interrupting me."

"Okay. Once they stop interrupting, what are we going to do?" she repeated, her hushed voice growing more frantic by the moment. "We can't let them think you're Mac!"

"I know! I don't know." Buck shook his head in exasperation. "Give me a minute, will you? I sure as heck didn't expect them to come driving up and catch us kissing—"

Holly looked around mortified. "Shh! Your parents might hear."

"Well," Buck huffed, and tore at his hair with frenzied fingers, "they're going to find out eventually."

"Ohhh," Holly moaned, releasing his shirt and wringing her hands. "I just didn't want them to find out this way. I mean, just look at them. They're all so happy. The truth would kill them. Let's at least let them have a few minutes to get reacquainted and enjoy one anothers' company before we drop the bomb on them.''

"Yeah. Okay. That sounds…sounds—'' Buck viciously rubbed at the tense muscles behind his neck "—completely insane. But, at the moment, I can't think of a better plan.''

Luckily they were spared having to make an immediate decision by Big Daddy's less than subtle proclamation that, "Everything is ready back in the courtyard, so come on!''

"Uh-oh,'' Buck groaned as they proceeded to follow their four giddy parents to the other side of the mansion.

"What, uh-oh?'' Holly asked anxiously as they dropped back and let the four excitedly chattering seniors lead the way along the path, past the tidy rows of box hedges and through the arbor that lead to the courtyard in the center of the formal gardens.

"Fasten your seat belt. I think that we're in for a bit of turbulence.''

"More turbulence?'' she echoed weakly.

Grim faced, Buck nodded. "I have a funny feeling there's some kind of party brewing back there.''

"What?'' she squeaked, and unconsciously clutched his strong hand for support. "Noooo. Not another party.''

Bringing up the rear, Holly and Buck woodenly passed through the ornate white arbor that was heavy with fragrant prize roses and into the courtyard proper. Like the eerie silence before a hurricane, not a word was spoken as they entered the area, secluded by hedges and tall iron gates. Not even a bird twittered. Then, as their parents stepped aside—revealing the gaily festooned and elaborately decorated courtyard—a paralyzing cacophony that

Holly would remember for the remainder of her days on this earth shattered her ears.

"Surprise!" came the deafening cry. "Congratulations, Holly!"

"Well, come on in, Holly! You, too, son," George commanded, roughly propelling Buck before him. "You're not gettin' off the hook that easily! If I gotta suffer through this girly shindig, you do too, son. So don't just stand there! Join the festivities. After all—" he winked at the two shocked young people he clutched by the shoulder "—it's in your honor!"

Trudy's head bobbed excitedly. "I've been planning this little co-ed bridal shower for weeks. That's why I wanted you to think we were coming down next week, instead of today."

Buck and Holly exchanged stupefied glances.

After the shouting had died down, the band struck a crashing chord and rolled into a song that seemed written expressly for the occasion:

"Happy shower, happy shower, Holly dear!
As your wedding day grows near
It's time to shower you with loving care,
And help the bride-to-be prepare
With necessities like flannel underwear!
And if your man gets out of hand
We know you'll need a fryin' pan!
So happy shower, happy shower, Holly dear!

Holly tightened her death grip on Buck's hand as the song rolled into several more grating verses filled with double entendre that would have been delightful under other circumstances.

Blankly, her eyes moved with Buck's around the smil-

ing crowd that packed the cobblestone courtyard. Everyone had come to celebrate in their good fortune, it
seemed. All the Brubaker kids, a multitude of neighbors
and old friends from the area that knew the Fergusons
from before they moved to Oklahoma and even a few of
the ranch hands stood in a curious, ogling group toward
the back. Yes, everyone was there.

Everyone, that is, with the glaring exception of the
groom.

"Make yourselves at home over there," Big Daddy
instructed the Ferguson family with a wave of his stubby
arm toward the head table.

Forcing her legs to carry her through the chaos, Holly
peered beseechingly over her shoulder at Buck and whispered, "I can't go through with this! It's not fair!"

"Well, you can't just quit now. It would hurt too many
people," Buck muttered under his breath. "It looks like
the folks went to a lot of trouble, putting this thing together."

"Ohh. I know." She groaned, glancing around as she
moved between the smiling guests. "Why didn't you tell
me about this?"

"Because I didn't know, either," he whispered between his teeth, his plastic smile pasted firmly on his face
as he followed her. Sarcasm tinged his words as he muttered under his breath. "I guess they figured that since I
was your personal cruise director on this ill-fated "Love
Boat" type summer of yours, their secret would be safer
if they didn't tell me."

"So I see," Holly responded, through her own brittle
smile. "Oh, look," she breathed through her clenched
teeth as she paused for a moment, first nodding at Bru
and Penelope, then letting her gaze land just beyond.

"Rhonda's here. And—" her eyes wandered disdainfully to Rhonda's large, open purse "—Precious, too."

"Precious doesn't look too happy to be here," Buck commented, pinching the bridge of his nose as Rhonda struggled to soothe her sensitive pet.

"I know exactly how the little varmint feels," Holly muttered as she continued to thread her way to the table Big Daddy had indicated. "Just keep her off my throat, will you?"

"Don't worry." Buck allowed himself a tight grin, beginning to see a glimmer of humor in the situation. "I think she prefers my neck for some reason."

"Oh, yoo-hoo! Holly!" Rhonda yodeled from her seat near the head of the table of honor. "Come sit over here by me! I can't wait till you see what Precious and Bootsie and I got you!" She clapped her hands enthusiastically, causing Precious to cower in a state of near catatonia. Holly had seen that look on the animal's face before. It always meant trouble.

Not knowing what else to do, Holly shrugged helplessly and left Buck's side to take her place of honor at the head of the long gift-lined table, next to Rhonda. Weaving their way through the masses of well-wishers, George and Trudy finally caught up with Buck and nudged him toward their daughter as she settled in next to Rhonda. As politely as possible, Buck resisted their less than subtle pressure and hung back, gesturing for Trudy to precede him.

"Well?" Big Daddy roared into the microphone that he'd had set up on a special little podium in the middle of the head table just for the occasion. "Holly, my new daughter-in-law-to-be, how about this? It's a co-ed bridal shower! It was your mother's idea. Were you surprised?"

"Ohhhhh, yessss," she breathed, her voice quavering

as she gripped the armrests of her chair and tentatively leaned back. "Very surprised."

"Well, good!" Big Daddy crowed. "That was the whole idea. To surprise you and your intended—" for a brief moment, Big Daddy allowed his eyes to anxiously sweep the crowd, hoping against hope that Mac would magically appear "—wherever he is," he muttered under his breath.

"We're right here!" George bellowed, and threw a meaty arm around Buck's shoulders. "Come on, son, don't be shy. Come take a load off, over here. You can sit by me, where we can get a good view of the proceedings." Not one to stand on ceremony, George thrust Buck before him like a battering ram into the thick of the crowd and pulled up several chairs front and center, near his daughter. "Trudy, honey! This way! Over here, darlin'! Come sit with me and son, here."

Eager to begin the proceedings, Trudy battled her way to her husband's side, her giddy laughter echoing around the courtyard. "Oh, that's a wonderful idea! Sit right here, between us, son!" she suggested, patting the empty seat and tugging on Buck's sleeve.

"I, uh…" Buck looked helplessly at Holly, who slumped in her chair and pressed her temples between her hands. Shrugging in resignation, Buck slid low into his seat and tried to look as inconspicuous as possible.

"Okay," Big Daddy hollered into his microphone, "let the celebratin' begin. Champagne will shortly be making the rounds, and the band will play for your listening pleasure. Now, if Holly would like to begin opening her presents, we will have some toasts and speeches for the bride when the cake is served a little later."

The crowd responded with the appropriate ooh's and aah's and twitters of delight as the waiters began serving the bubbly, and the band began a litany of love songs that made Holly want to scream.

"Open mine first," Rhonda gushed, and, pulling her gift off the pile, thrust it into Holly's hands. Shooting Buck a coy look she simpered, "Every woman should have one of these on her wedding night!"

"Oh. I, uh, thank you," Holly stammered, and with downcast eyes proceeded to open it, the first of literally hundreds of gifts. "Ohh, my gracious sakes," she murmured as she lifted the filmy scrap of lacy black silk out of the box and let it dangle between her fingertips.

"It's a garter belt!" Rhonda gushed, and, snatching it out of Holly's hands, stood and demonstrated where it should ride on the hips. Pelvis undulating, she batted coquettish lashes at Buck.

"Whooo lawsy!" George hooted, and waved a meaty fist. "I bet you can't wait to get a load of her in that!" he cried, playfully punching Buck on his shoulder as he pointed at Rhonda. "Maybe these co-ed shindigs are more fun than we thought, right, son?"

Puzzled smiles were exchanged over George's curious remarks, then laughed off as boisterous party talk.

"Oh, George," Trudy chided with an explosion of embarrassed laughter. "Try to behave."

"What?" His chin doubled as he leaned back and arched an innocent brow at his wife. "We're just having a little fun."

Reaching over Holly, Rhonda snatched the matching bra out of the remaining tissue in Holly's hands and stretched it over her own healthy cleavage. "This goes with it," she announced as she swayed to and fro, her bosom heaving dramatically. "This should bring Mac a runnin', don't you think?"

"I, uh…" Holly glanced at Precious who, shying away

from her master's wildly swaying hips, looked more likely to run than anyone.

"Sheew-ee!" George cackled, and slapped Buck on the back. "What do you think, boy? That skimpy little thing get your engines runnin'?" His exuberant laughter echoed around the courtyard, drawing more stares. Some curious. Some scandalized.

"Oh, no, sir, I..." Buck stammered, trying to appear nonchalant even as his heart threatened to burst out of his rib cage. "What I mean..."

"George!" Trudy scolded, and, chuckling, patted Buck on the knee. "You're embarrassing him."

"Oh, Tommy rot, Trudy! He's a big boy. Gonna be married one day soon. He can handle it."

Rhonda's eyes widened, a mixture of expectant emotions flitting across her pretty face as she stretched Holly's skimpy new bra to its breaking point. "Married?" she whispered, looking questioningly at Buck.

"Not for a while," Buck hedged, and shook his head slightly at her, then darted a miserable glance at Holly.

"That's okay," Rhonda said, trying to conceal her rabid curiosity. "You can tell me later."

As Holly continued to doggedly work her way through the stacks of lacy lingerie, George continued to holler and catcall in a fashion that proved to everyone present that this was indeed his first bridal shower, and the more delicate etiquette of the occasion was lost on him. Soon, however, the ranch hands joined in, woofing and hooting with carefree, raucous abandon, piping down only when they caught the murder in their boss's eyes.

When after nearly a torturous half hour, blushing madly, Holly held up yet another skimpy garment meant for her wedding night, George could hold back no longer.

"Why, son," he sputtered, slapping Buck heartily on

his thigh. "She's gonna hafta put on a private little fashion show for you later on, huh? I bet you can't wait to see her in all those different getups, know what I mean?"

The crowd gasped.

Rhonda's head snapped around in shock.

"George! Our daughter is not married yet!" Trudy sputtered, her ever-present laughter was more the mortified variety now.

Throwing his hands up in the air, George pooh-poohed his wife's puritan attitudes. "Oh, for heaven's sake, Trudy! We're all adults, here. Good grief, she's going to be a married woman soon. Time to stop babying her. Why, in this day and age, I'd be surprised if these two hadn't already spent some time behind the wood shed just to work out the kinks, if you know what I mean!" His loud guffaw met stony silence. "What'd I say?" he asked, jerking his head back and forth as he glanced around at the stunned faces of the guests.

"Well, now." Big Daddy cleared his throat into the microphone and drew his furry brows together in a slightly puzzled frown. "George, old friend, you oughta know by now that's not exactly the way it works in my family. There's no hanky-panky before the weddin'. Ever. And this boy here—" he pointed at Buck, who was now slowly shaking his head at Holly "—well, he thinks of Miss Holly here as a sister!"

Buck closed his eyes and rubbed his throbbing temples.

"Sister?" George snorted. "Big Daddy, you always did have such a great sense of humor. Boy howdy, I've missed you. Now you can't tell me that you've raised a bunch of monks! These are healthy boys here, and I could tell by the way he was kissin' my daughter, when we drove up, that there's a heck of a fire roarin' between these two.''

"*What?*" Rhonda leapt to her feet. "You were kissing *Holly?*" she shrieked. The unexpected movement and the ensuing gasps from the crowd were poor, petrified Precious's undoing. Completely unhinged, the freaked-out ferret escaped the confines of her mistress's purse and began her frantic scramble over the mountain of shower presents to begin her own amazing wilderness trek.

"Rat!" one woman screamed, pointing a shaking finger at the bug-eyed Precious. "EEEEEeeeeeekkkkk!"

"Rat! Rat!" came the answering cry from lovely Southern belles, dressed in all manner of delicate finery. Hats flopping, purses flapping, skirts flipping, the bridal shower guests squealed in terror.

"My land," Miss Clarise murmured, gazing at her third son as he bolted from his seat and followed the sobbing Holly out of the courtyard as fast as her wobbly legs could carry her.

Soon the clamor of an already excited shower party swelled into the mutinous hue and cry of a fledgling riot as it tried to capture and contain one small, frightened ferret.

"It's not a rat!" another woman screamed. "It's a flying squirrel! And it's in the cake! Quick! Get it!"

"Ohh! Not the blamed cake," the ranch hand named Fuzzy grumbled, jumping up onto the serving table to capture the wily Precious before she could sully the dessert.

The screechings and hissings of audio feedback pierced the air as Big Daddy grabbed his microphone and pointed it at his dearest old friend. "George Ferguson!" he boomed, attempting to be heard above the complete and total bedlam that ensued. "What do you mean when you say my son was kissin' your daughter?"

"What's the big deal?" George wondered aloud, dodging a cake-covered Precious as she streaked past in her pursuit of freedom.

"The big deal is—" Big Daddy sighed and gave his head a puzzled scratch "—that boy's not her fiancé. That boy's Buck. My third son."

George, his grin sagging like a punctured balloon, squinted over at Big Daddy who, still standing in the eye of the bridal hurricane, looked equally as shell-shocked as his friend. "Will someone please tell me what the hell is going on around here?" George blustered to no one in particular

"I'm not sure," Big Daddy ranted, "but I sure as heck aim to get to the bottom of it. Come on, George. Let's go find out!"

A wild roar went up from the delighted and curious crowd. Once again, the Brubakers had come through with an excellent party. The country band struck up a rousing chorus of the "Holly Shower Song" as the chaos escalated. Dodging assorted hats, gloves, pocketbooks and bits of shower cake, Big Daddy wove through the brawling mob—George Ferguson and Precious the ferret hot on his heels—and out of the courtyard in search of Buck and Holly.

"You were *never* engaged to him?" Buck stared incredulously at Holly as her devastating words began to sink in.

"No."

Pushing off the swing that he'd been sharing with her in the old Victorian gazebo, he whirled to face her, his jaw grimly set, his eyes steely. Backing slowly away, he planted his hands low on his hips and commanded himself to count to ten before he spoke again. When he did speak, he chose his words carefully. "All summer long, you've been pretending to be engaged to Mac?"

"Yes." Eyes downcast, Holly's whispered words were barely audible.

Plunging a hand through his hair, he shook his head, trying his best to understand. "But why didn't you tell me what was going on?"

"Because I promised."

"Even though you knew how I felt about you?"

"But I *didn't* know how you felt."

Buck narrowed his gaze at her.

"Not until later," she amended, bringing her large liquid eyes to his.

"But you lied. Both of you. All damn summer long, you lied to all of us. Mom, Big Daddy, all the kids and—" he expelled all the hurt in his belly with a long groan "—me."

"I didn't *want* to lie to you, Buck." Holly's lower lip began to tremble.

"But you did." Fury sparked in his eyes as he moved over to a porch post and slapped it with the broad side of his hand. "You could have told me the truth. You knew how I felt about you. You could have trusted me. But you didn't." His low voice rose a notch as his anger grew. "After everything we've been through this summer, you didn't trust me."

"But I do."

"Then why the hell didn't you tell me before now?" he demanded, furiously pushing off the post and striding over to stand directly before her. He crossed his arms across his chest because he ached to haul her into his arms and kiss away her obvious dilemma, and at the same time, he wanted to turn her over his knee and paddle her shapely little derriere. But he could do neither.

"I couldn't, don't you see? Mac made me promise not to tell anyone," she cried, frightened at the restrained look of fury on his face. "It all started out as a practical joke, and then it just kind of got out of control from there," she struggled to explain as his eyes slowly hardened into glittering coals of fury. "Then...then...Mac, he had to leave right away. For personal reasons, and he *swore* me to secrecy, and I *had* to help him! Because...because I owed him..." Her voice trailed off miserably.

"So." His jaw twitched as he contemplated her words. "This whole summer was nothing more than one big practical joke to you."

"No! It's not like that," Holly cried, her face haunted with grief over the endless trouble she knew her little scheme with Mac would spawn. "You're making it sound much worse than it is! You don't understand!"

"Make me understand! Make me understand how you could lie to me all summer, knowing how I felt about you. Knowing that I was falling head over heels in...in...*love*—" he spat this word as if it had suddenly become a vile taste in his mouth "—with you!"

Feeling too tortured to continue this discussion, Buck spun on his heel, reached back and punched the porch post for all he was worth, bringing back a bruised hand for his effort. He wished it was Mac's face and not the post he was pummeling, but that would have to wait until his favorite brother ever got around to coming home.

"Buck..." Hands reaching out to him, her face shattered, Holly leaned forward in the swing and whispered his name. "Buck..."

"I gotta go."

"Buck." Holly sobbed. "Please wait."

"I've waited long enough," he said over his shoulder.

And with that, he bounded down the stairs, two at a time, left the gazebo without a backward glance and headed toward the barn to grab a mount and work off some of his fury. Fury at being duped by Holly. By his brother. Fury at not being able to see the truth from the beginning.

She'd been stringing him along all summer. Playing him for a fool.

Well, that was exactly what he was. A royal fool. Reaching the stable, he saddled his fastest horse and instinctively headed out to the South Section, to the spot where he'd first kissed his brother's woman.

Feeling utterly wretched, Holly leaned forward in the swing and sobbed. A keening wail racked her body as her heart finally shattered. Buck was gone. Her parents would be furious with her, not to mention the entire Brubaker family. Tears flowed down her cheeks, and for the first time in her life, Holly wished that an errant bolt of lightning would strike her dead. For how could she go on living without Buck? Endless moments passed as she cried, grinding her fists into her eyes to stem the flow of hopeless emotion, and wishing she had a tissue to mop the waterworks that it seemed would never cease.

"Holly?" a gentle voice asked just over her shoulder.

She stiffened as the weight of a human body settled into the swing next to her. Blinded by tears, she struggled to make out the familiar face that peered into her own. "Buck?" she asked, smiling with relief.

"No, it's me. Mac."

"Mac?" she cried, sitting up straight, suddenly furious. *"Mac?"* she shrieked, squaring her shoulders, and, without ceremony, hauled off and slugged him in the stomach.

Chapter Nine

"There they are!" Big Daddy huffed, pointing the way as he trotted across the lawn toward the gazebo. Charging headfirst, he lead not only George, but Trudy and Miss Clarise, as well. "They're in the gazebo!" came Big Daddy's battle cry.

"Wait up, now, Big Daddy," George thundered, laboriously lumbering after his old buddy. "I have a thing or two I want to say to these kids myself," he panted as they finally reached and stormed the gazebo.

Big Daddy, being the first to stumble up the stairs, screeched to a stop and stared in confusion at the young couple who stood squared off in front of the swings. "Mac?" he asked confused. "Bu-but where's Buck?"

Holly lifted tear-filled eyes to Big Daddy. "He's gone."

"Gone?"

"Yes."

"For good?" the old man bellowed in disbelief.

"Ohhh," Holly sobbed. "I don't know. Maybe. Probably." Despondently, she slid back down into the swing and buried her head in her hands.

Big Daddy dug a handkerchief out of his pocket and, with a sorrowful shake of his head, handed it to Holly. "Not another disappearin' son! I can't take much more of this. I got a ranch and a handful of businesses to run. I can't have you blasted boys takin' off whenever it strikes your fancy." He scowled at Mac. "Where the devil you been?"

"That's what I'd like to know, young man," George demanded, trundling into the gazebo behind Big Daddy.

"It's a long story, Big Daddy. One that I should probably tell you later on." Mac nodded apologetically at George and Trudy. "In private."

"In *private*?" Big Daddy thundered his exasperation. "All hell broke loose while you were gone, boy!" Slowly, the old man shook his head as he regarded the serious expression on his son's face. "Well, all I gotta say is, it better be good!"

Holly pressed the back of her hand to her pounding temple. "Oh, it is. You can trust me on that much."

Mac smiled broadly in spite of himself.

"Good, good, good," Big Daddy shouted, grabbed his son by the arm. "Now that you're back, sit yourself down with your woman here, and sort out this mess you made by disappearin' for so long. Then I want you and Holly to set a weddin' date."

"Nooo," Holly moaned, and noisily blew her nose into Big Daddy's monogrammed handkerchief.

"No?" George demanded, completely flabbergasted by now. "No? What do you mean, no?"

"No?" Big Daddy said. "What does that mean, no?"

"No!" Holly cried.

"What in thunder is going on around here?" George blustered.

"Yes," cried Big Daddy, "what is going on?"

Miss Clarise battled her way up the stairs and stomped her tiny foot until both men looked at her. "Let's leave Mac and Holly alone for a few moments so that they can sort out their problems. Now!" she yelled, poking Big Daddy in the chest with a furious finger.

Big Daddy looked over his shoulder at George and grinned. "I just love it when she's frisky."

With a bawdy hoot, George ambled down the stairs after Trudy and Miss Clarise and went off to join the party.

At long last, Mac and Holly were finally alone. His hat in his hands, Mac gestured to the spot next to Holly on the swing. "Mind if I join you?"

"Suit yourself."

"Promise you won't hit me again?" Peering down into her face, he grinned.

Holly sniffed, and a tiny smile flirted with the corners of her mouth. "I can't make any promises. You'll have to sit at your own risk."

Mac chuckled. "I guess I can do that," he said, and slowly lowered his lanky frame into the spot next to her.

Swallowing past the lump in her throat, Holly sniffed and looked curiously at him. "So. Where the hell have you been for the past three weeks?" she grumbled.

With a heartfelt sigh, Mac reached over and took Holly's hand into his and squeezed. "On a mission of discovery so wonderful it would take all day to tell you about it. For now, just suffice it to say that I am probably the happiest man in the world."

"At least someone is."

"You're not, I take it?"

Tears welled anew into her eyes. "No," she choked miserably.

"Care to tell Uncle Mac the problem?" His voice, so sympathetic and full of caring and so very much like his brother's, was Holly's undoing.

"Oh, Mac," she sobbed. "It's such a mess."

"It was rough on you, keeping the secret all by yourself?"

"Uh-huh..." She sniffed. "It was horrible! And wrong! Very wrong, Mac!" Turning in her seat, she cast her watery gaze to him. "I had to lie to everyone that I love. Your parents, my parents, all your brothers...and especially...Buck."

"Buck?" An interested light filled his eyes.

"Yes. Oh, Mac, your father insisted that Buck take care of me while you were gone. He didn't mean to, Mac, but he kind of...well, he sort of..."

"Fell in love with you?"

"Yes." She sighed, crumpling against the back of the swing.

"I had a funny feeling about that, before I left to go find my wife," he mused with a smile. Turning, he regarded the blotchy-faced Holly. "And you fell in love with him, too?"

"Yes," she whispered, the huge tears that had pooled on her lower lashes spilled over and splashed on her tightly clasped hands. "Yes, I love him. With all my heart."

A poignant smile tinged Mac's lips. "And you had to pretend to be in love with me, because I swore you to secrecy."

"Ye-ye-yessss," she blubbered, and buried her face in her handkerchief.

"Oh, sweetheart." Mac sighed, and, leaning back in

the swing, put a comforting arm around Holly's delicate shoulders as they were racked with sobs. "I'm so sorry. I had no idea that you were going through all this. I wasn't thinking about anybody else but myself."

Now she could understand quite clearly how one could forget to act like a decent human being when the threat of losing one you love was involved. She'd done it all summer.

"Do you forgive me?"

Sighing, Holly nodded again and sagged against the comforting warmth of his strong body.

"Good." He sighed. "Because I couldn't have my future sister-in-law all mad at me now, could I?"

"Sister-in-law?" Holly asked dully.

"Well, I suspect when that dunderheaded brother of mine hears the whole story, he'll forgive us and beg you to marry him."

"Somehow I doubt that," Holly stated flatly.

"Now, now," Mac said, and kissed the side of her forehead in a brotherly manner. "You just leave that to me. You see, he owes me a pretty big favor for—"

"I know, I know," Holly murmured, closing her eyes and allowing a small smile to steal across her face. "For pulling his sorry hide out of a cow tank when you were kids."

"Ah, so you've heard." Mac chuckled, giving her shoulder a comforting pat.

"I know everything there is to know about Buck Brubaker." Holly sighed.

Buck reigned his sweating mount to a stop near the pond where he and Holly had gone swimming several weeks ago. Leaping to the ground, he led his horse to water and, dipping his hat into the cool, clear liquid, managed to douse his own hot head.

Hotheaded. That's what he was all right, he thought self-deprecatingly. As the water sluiced off his head and soaked his shirt, he stood, brushing the water out of his eyes with his sleeve, and silently cursed himself.

He hadn't really even given Holly a chance to explain why Mac had left so suddenly last month. He hadn't really wanted to know, fearing it might interfere with his plans to have Holly all to himself. She'd been trying to apologize for her part in what must have been a practical joke gone wrong, but he hadn't listened.

And why not?

Hadn't he been caught in the exact same kind of dilemma when George and Trudy wouldn't allow him to explain who he really was? It had been much easier to go with the flow, not risking hurting their exuberant feelings, than to drop a bomb like that on them. Slowly Buck was beginning to understand a little of what Holly must have been going through this summer.

It had to have been hard on her, keeping up this ruse all by herself for the sake of his miserable brother. Especially if she was beginning to have feelings for himself.

As these simple realizations dawned, Buck's anger began to dissipate. In its place, a compassion began to swell in his heart. He loved this woman. Maybe he didn't think that she and Mac should have pulled the stunt they did, but then he didn't really know what they were up against at the time, either.

Slowly Buck reshaped his damp hat and propped it back on his head. Gathering the reins to his mount, he swung into his saddle and, with a subtle clicking sound, nudged his horse into first a trot, then a gentle lope, then, as his urgency to see Holly and hear the rest of her story grew, a full-blown gallop.

"Wow," Holly murmured as she and Mac continued to languidly swing back and forth in the old Victorian gazebo. "You really had quite the summer."

"Yeah," Mac agreed, ruffling her hair with his hand and smiling into her eyes. "Just about as exciting as yours, from the sound of it."

Catching his hand in her own, Holly smiled ruefully and impulsively kissed him on the cheek. "Thank you."

"For what?" Mac asked, his voice sounding decidedly drowsy.

"For telling me everything." She sighed. "Somehow, it makes everything I went through this summer seem worthwhile."

"Honey," Mac said, giving her shoulder a playful squeeze, "if you love my brother even half as much as I think you do, your summer was worth it. Practical jokes, bitter fights, public scandal and—" he sighed tiredly "—all."

"Hmm," Holly said, smiling. "We'll...see... about—" Lifting her head slightly from the back of the swing, she looked at Mac, her smile slowly fading. "Do you hear that?"

Mac listened. "Sounds like a horse."

"Yeah," Holly said with a frown. "And it's moving pretty fast!"

"And toward us!"

Mac sat up just in time to see his brother come flying up on his horse, yank the reins to a screeching stop and vault off the animal's back over the ornate Victorian railing and into the gazebo.

Yelling like a banshee for all he was worth, Buck

grabbed his older brother and hauled him out of the swing where he'd been sitting so cozily with Holly.

His Holly.

Yeah, he'd seen the kissing and hand-holding. The little smiles and the chummy hugs. He'd seen it all, but that didn't mean he had to like it.

"There you are, you rotten, lowlife, good for nothing—" Buck ranted, murder in his eyes as he gripped his surprised brother by the front of his shirt and dragged him out of the swing and to his feet "—son of a—" Bam! Right fist connected with left jaw, and Mac fell to the ground.

"Buck, stop!" Holly screamed as Buck reached down and grabbed his reeling brother and hauled him back up to his uncooperative feet.

"Holly, stay out of this," Buck ordered through his tightly clenched teeth, propping his brother up for another long-awaited punch in the face. "This is between me and my dear brother."

Woozily, Mac rubbed his aching jaw and shook his head. "Now wait just a darn minute, little brother," he cautioned, taking a wobbly step back and lifting his hands to defend himself.

"I've waited all damn summer to do this," Buck roared, scoring another right cross to Mac's already bruised and swollen face, then lunging at his brother and dragging him to the ground.

There, for what seemed like an eternity, they grappled, rolling around, shouting like lunatics and punching each other, getting up, and dragging each other back down, and rolling around some more.

"Buck, please," Holly begged, wringing her hands.

"Holly, stay out of this," Mac ordered. "I can handle him... Ouch, dammit!"

"Shut up, Mac. You don't have any right to tell her what to do, you sniveling—uhf—wimp." Buck grunted, digging his brother's fingers out of his face. "You didn't...even have the decency to—uhhg—call Holly the entire time you were gone! Don't you think—ouch—she had a hard time keeping up your end of this harebrained bargain?" Grabbing Mac by the throat, he rolled over and straddled him. "Where the hell have you been? How could you leave such a wonderful woman here, all alone, to deal with your lousy lies?"

"I—" Mac huffed, prying his brother's fingers from around his windpipe. Kicking Buck away from him, he tried desperately to stand. "I already told her why I had to go!"

"Buck! Mac! Stop it!" Holly shrieked, jumping out of their way as they made it to an upright position only to come flying across the gazebo floor to land at her feet.

"And why is that—" Buck panted "—you lily-livered coward? Were you tired of lying to everyone and decided to take a powder?" Grabbing Mac by his ankles as he tried to stand, Buck managed to drag him back to the ground and get in a few more licks.

"No!" Mac groaned, struggling to get out from under his brother. "I...had...to go find...my...wife."

Nonplussed, Buck stilled for a moment, completely winded, and simply stared at his brother's ankles. "Your what?" he asked dully, turning around and peering into his brother's eyes.

Flopping back on his back, Mac dabbed at one of the numerous bleeding cuts on his face with the sleeve of his shirt and sighed. "My wife."

"Your wife?" Buck snorted skeptically.

"Mmm-hmm."

Buck stared at him agog. "You're married?"

"Yep. For almost a year."

"A year?"

"Yeah. We eloped a few months after Bru and Penelope got married. Anyway, when she ran off—" He opened one weary eye and trained it at his brother. "Don't ask. It's a very, very long and complicated story. Anyway, I needed a handy cover to keep Big Daddy from meddling in my private affairs while I looked for her. Holly very graciously volunteered to help me out by posing as my fiancée. That way, Big Daddy would stop fixing me up with women I couldn't date, and it gave me time to look for my wife, without a bunch of interference from our wonderful, well-meaning parents."

Buck blinked and shook his head as he slowly sat up and looked at his brother. "You've been married for almost a *year?* And you didn't tell anyone?"

"I couldn't. I didn't even tell Holly the whole story until just a few minutes ago. Didn't want to blow my chances of finding her again. Later, when we have more time, and I'm not feeling quiet so—" he winced and dabbed at the bleeding cut above his eye "—thrashed, I'll give you all the details. But for now—" he sighed and groaned wearily "—I'm going to go find my wife and an ice pack or two. Man," Mac grumbled as he slowly hauled himself to his feet and regarded the couple in front of him. "You both pack a pretty mean wallop. I can see now that you are perfect for each other." Grinning as broadly as his swollen eye and lip would allow, he held his hand out to Buck. "I'm sorry, buddy. I had no idea what I was putting you two through these past few weeks." He looked earnestly back and forth between them both. "Please. Forgive me."

Rolling his eyes, Buck shrugged and grasped his

brother's hand. "Yeah, well, we're even now, for you pulling my sorry hide out of the cow tank."

Mac's grin was lopsided. "Congratulations, brother. You've got a winner." After a hearty handshake, he released Buck's hand and pulled Holly close. "Give me a kiss, sis," he demanded. "For old time's sake." And with that, he dipped Holly back and planted a quick, hard, kiss on her mouth. "Yep," he drawled, setting her upright and ambling out of the gazebo to leave them alone. "Yes, indeedy, brother dear," he drawled over his shoulder. "I'd have given you a run for your money."

Frozen where he stood, Buck watched his brother limp across the lawn and finally disappear into the house. Then, slowly, he angled his head and, looking across the gazebo at Holly, whispered, "Would he?"

"Would he what?"

"Have given me a run for my money?" His face was vulnerable, the light of hope and love in his eyes.

"Never." Her whispered word was a vow. "I love you. Only you."

"I love you, too." Buck sighed and, taking one long step across the old wooden floor, grabbed Holly. And for the first time in their relationship, he hauled her into his arms and kissed her as his woman. The kiss was soft and filled with myriad emotions that could finally be expressed in this special way.

"You do?" she breathed after a long, dizzying moment. "Even after everything we've been through this summer? Even after all the lies I told?"

"Yes, even then."

"Oh, Buck. For so long, I've wanted to tell you the truth. To tell you how sorry I am and to ask you to forgive me. I've hated hiding the truth from you this way.

Especially since it kept us apart, when I wanted so badly to be with you."

"I know, honey. You're forgiven. I'm not condoning what you and Mac did. But, in a way, I understand. Much better now, after that nutty bridal shower this afternoon." He shook his head as he kissed her neck. "I have to admit, your parents are just as pushy as mine."

"Mmm," Holly murmured, twining her hand behind his neck, loving the silky feeling of his hair. "Maybe more."

"But I think I can stand George and Trudy as my in-laws, if you can stand Big Daddy and Miss Clarise as yours."

Eyes flashing, Holly leaned back and looked up into Buck's handsome face, searching it for the true meaning of his words. "Are you saying what I think you're saying?"

"That I want to see you in all that lacy stuff on our wedding night?" Groaning, he kissed her hard and long on the mouth. "Yep." He moaned, leaning his forehead against hers. "That's exactly what I'm saying."

"When?" she asked excitedly.

"The sooner, the better," Buck said, filling his hands with the wonderful, silky soft hair he'd admired from afar for the whole first half of the summer. "Some of that stuff was very interesting. Very interesting," he growled, nipping the shell of her ear with his teeth and lips.

Holly giggled. "Rhonda will be disappointed."

"Nah." Buck shook his head. "She already has a family of her own. Now it's our turn."

For a long time, they stood there, holding each other close in a tender embrace, gently kissing, taking time to explore the softer side of their relationship. The side that was guilt free, and sanctioned by each other and, most especially, Mac.

"Buck?"

"Hmm?"

"What about Miracle House?" As far as Holly was concerned, that was part of her family, too..

"Well, you know, I've been thinking about that…"

"You have?"

"Mmm-hmm." Buck nodded and lead her to the swing where he pulled her onto his lap. "I have a little piece of land—just a few hundred acres—not too far from here that would make a terrific ranch for needy kids. If you want, we could think about donating it to Miracle House. They could set up another division here in Texas."

"Really?" Holly breathed, her eyes shining with love for this wonderful, thoughtful man.

"Sure. If they wanted, I'd even be interested in helping them run it for a while."

"Really?" Cupping his face between her hands, Holly pressed her nose to Buck's. "You would do that for me?"

He nodded. "And for me. And for the kids. The kids on the ranch, and maybe for the one or two we might have ourselves."

"Oh, Buck," Holly murmured, tears of joy welling into her eyes. "I think you have just made me the happiest woman on the face of this earth."

"No," Buck said with a twinkle in his eye, "but I plan to. Soon."

And with that solemn promise, he angled Holly's mouth beneath his and began to show her what he meant.

Epilogue

Much to Buck and Holly's amazement, the bridal shower was still in full swing in the courtyard, many hours later. Evening had come, filling the giant Texas sky with a brilliant scattering of glittering stars. The soft, warm late-summer breeze wafted through the gardens, sending a light floral scent flitting into the air. From the bandstand, the music of Big Daddy's heart flowed, entertaining the still surprisingly crowded courtyard. The dance floor was filled to bursting. Of course, Big Daddy and Miss Clarise were swaying to the sultry love tunes, as were George and Trudy and Bru and Penelope.

Buck and Holly had lingered in the gazebo, making exciting plans for their future, and reveling in the opportunity to kiss and snuggle to their heart's desire, without fear of breaking some horrendous moral code. Finally, as the shadows had crept across the lawn, pulling the darkening sky behind them, the young couple decided it was time to break the news to their parents. While they were at it, it seemed prudent to kill several birds with one stone and tell the curious shower guests what was going on, as well.

Leading Holly through the gaily partying crowd, Buck moved to the podium and tapped the microphone. "Ahem," he said, and tapped some more, hoping to capture everyone's attention. The band took the cue and eventually stopped playing.

"Hello," Buck began, and pulled Holly closely to his side as he attempted to explain. "I know a lot of you came here today to celebrate the bridal shower of Holly Ferguson, thinking that she was going to marry my brother Mac." Glancing at Holly, he cleared his throat and looked out across the sea of curious, smiling faces. "Well, we just wanted you to know that Holly and Mac will not be getting married, after all."

A collective gasp filled the courtyard. Mutterings and mumblings rumbled amongst the guests as they speculated about this new turn of events.

"What in thunder are you saying, boy?" Big Daddy wanted to know from where he stood on the dance floor.

"Well, I guess what I'm trying to tell you is that Holly will be getting married. Just not to Mac."

"To who, then?" George wanted to know.

"To me."

"To *you?* But...but...I thought..." Big Daddy cried, just before his eyes rolled back in his head and he fell to the floor in a dead faint.

"Oh, my," Miss Clarise gasped. "Not again!" Looking to George for assistance, she fanned her husband's pale face and helped her friend prop him up. "He does this every time one of the kids announces that they are going to be married."

Rushing to Big Daddy's side, Buck and Holly knelt down beside him and patted his hands.

"Big Daddy, are you going to be okay?" Buck asked, pulling off his father's hat and loosening his tie.

"Well, I guess so, just as soon as I figure out what's goin' on around here. What about Mac? In fact, where is Mac?"

"I think he had a headache and turned in early," Buck explained with a small smile at Holly. "But you don't have to worry about him, Big Daddy. He already told us that he has no intention of marrying Holly."

"Really?" Puzzled, Big Daddy looked back and forth between Holly and Buck. "Well, I sure as hell don't get it, pardon my French, honey, but if y'all are happy, then I'm happy. Congratulations!"

The crowd let loose with a lengthy round of good-natured cheering and well-wishing.

Struggling to his feet with the help of Buck and Holly, Big Daddy eyed the pair that stood before him. "You're sure Mac's okay with all this?"

Holly nodded. "More than okay, sir. Truthfully, we were never really suited."

"Well," George blustered. "I guess it's better that you find out now, before you marry the wrong brother." Swallowing, and dabbing at a suspicious bit of moisture in his eyes, he grabbed his daughter and kissed her cheeks. "I only ever wanted for you to be happy, honey."

"Yes, Daddy. I know," Holly murmured, giving her father a loving squeeze. "And I am. Very happy."

"Then," George boomed to the overtly eavesdropping guests, "all I can say is—" he reached for a lacy scrap from the gift table "—I bet you can hardly wait to see her in this!"

"Oh, George," Trudy warbled, holding her sides against the laughter. "The things you say."

Later that same night—after the party had finally fizzled—in the privacy of their own bedroom, Big Daddy and Miss Clarise sat toasting each other with champagne for another happy ending.

"Such a wonderful day," Miss Clarise enthused. "Buck and Holly are in love and getting married, and you're ending up with the daughter-in-law you always wanted even though she's not marrying the son you expected... Penelope and Bru are expecting a baby any moment... Oh, how wonderful!" Softly humming, she moved to her vanity and began to brush her hair.

"Yep," Big Daddy said, feeling greatly satisfied as he lit an expensive cigar and settled into an armchair. "You're right, sugar lips. Everything turned out just fine."

Miss Clarise paused, holding her brush in both hands and turned to look at her husband. "Big Daddy, did I see Ella in the kitchen earlier, visiting with the staff?"

"Yes, ma'am. And thank heavens. I've missed that gal this past year. Wonder why she ran off, and why she came back. Not that I mind her return. Nobody can cook like that girl." Big Daddy puffed a series of smoke rings and sighed with contentment. "Yep, honey pie, it's been a stellar day. I tell ya, none of this would have happened if I hadn't given those boys a little nudge. You know, darlin', now that Buck and Holly are tying the knot, maybe we oughta think about finding some nice girl for Mac," Big Daddy mused thoughtfully.

"Big Daddy," Miss Clarise said, dropping her brush and heading over to perch on the arm of her husband's chair. "You think too much," she murmured, and planted a tender kiss on his cheek.

*   *   *   *   *

So who did Mac marry, and how did he win her love? Get the story from the beginning when **THE BRUBAKER BRIDES** *continues. Look for* CINDERELLA'S SECRET BABY *coming in July 1998 from Carolyn Zane and Silhouette Romance.*

Take 4 bestselling love stories FREE

Plus get a FREE surprise gift!

CHRISTINE FLYNN

Continues the twelve-book series—36 HOURS—in December 1997 with Book Six

FATHER AND CHILD REUNION

Eve Stuart was back, and Rio Redtree couldn't ignore the fact that her daughter bore his Native American features. So, Eve had broken his heart *and* kept him from his child! But this was no time for grudges, because his little girl and her mother, the woman he had never stopped—could never stop—loving, were in danger, and Rio would stop at nothing to protect *his* family.

For Rio and Eve and *all* the residents of Grand Springs, Colorado, the storm-induced blackout was just the beginning of 36 Hours that changed *everything!* You won't want to miss a single book.

Welcome to the Towers!

In January
New York Times bestselling author

NORA ROBERTS

takes us to the fabulous Maine coast mansion
haunted by a generations-old secret and introduces
us to the fascinating family that lives there.

Mechanic Catherine "C.C." Calhoun and hotel magnate
Trenton St. James mix like axle grease and mineral
water—until they kiss. Efficient Amanda Calhoun finds
easygoing Sloan O'Riley insufferable—and irresistible.
And they all must race to solve the mystery
surrounding a priceless hidden emerald necklace.

Catherine and Amanda

THE Calhoun Women

**A special 2-in-1 edition containing
COURTING CATHERINE and A MAN FOR AMANDA.**

Look for the next installment of
THE CALHOUN WOMEN with Lilah and Suzanna's
stories, coming in March 1998.

Available at your favorite retail outlet.

Silhouette®

Return to the Towers!

In March
New York Times bestselling author

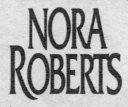

NORA ROBERTS

brings us to the Calhouns' fabulous
Maine coast mansion and reveals the
tragic secrets hidden there for generations.

For all his degrees, Professor Max Quartermain has a
lot to learn about love—and luscious Lilah Calhoun is
just the woman to teach him. Ex-cop Holt Bradford is
as prickly as a thornbush—until Suzanna Calhoun's
special touch makes love blossom in his heart.
And all of them are caught in the race to solve
the generations-old mystery of a priceless
lost necklace...and a timeless love.

Lilah and Suzanna
THE
Calhoun Women

A special 2-in-1 edition containing
FOR THE LOVE OF LILAH and
SUZANNA'S SURRENDER

Available at your favorite retail outlet.